I0621379

The Mummy's Twin

by G. H. Teed

Illustrated by Eric Parker

First published in the Union Jack magazine,
series 2, no. 1067, 22 March 1924.

Stillwoods Edition

Stillwoods.Blogspot.Ca

Catalogue Information:
Title: The Mummy's Twin
Author: G. H. Teed (1881-1938)
Illustrated by: Eric Parker
First published anonymously in the Union Jack magazine, series 2, no. 1067, 22 March 1924.
This Edition by: Stillwoods, 2021
ISBN Canada: 978-1-989788-67-7
Blog: Stillwoods.Blogspot.Ca
Author Blog: http://ghteed.blogspot.com/
Storefront: http://www.lulu.com/spotlight/lulubook22

Copyright © Doug Frizzle and/or Stillwoods, 2021.
Cover adapted from the original.

Teed Bibliography Link:
https://tinyurl.com/ve25d42s
The link above should go to a spreadsheet of all known Teed stories. The list is annotated with various information on the stories and my progress with recapturing the work.   /drf

The library of Teed's stories increases almost daily. Check at the storefront link above for the latest arrivals. /drf

Keywords: Sexton Blake, British fictional detective, Tinker, Prince Menes

Cautionary Note: This series of books by Stillwoods are intended to make the stories of G. H. Teed, born in New Brunswick, Canada, available to collectors and researchers. The editor, or rather digitizer has not intentionally altered the original publication.

This story may contain language and racial terms that are not appropriate to today. I apologize for them; I know that the author was using his voice to excite and entertain an adventurous English audience. These works were published from 82 to 110 years ago. Most every work has characters of redeeming ethnicity within.

I hope you enjoy and share these stories; I have.
Doug Frizzle

The MUMMY'S TWIN

Perhaps there is somebody somewhere who will not care for this story. If so, that person has a very pernickety taste. To those to whom the mysticism of Egypt's past appeals, or the scope of its adventure in the present, this yarn will have irresistible charm. Before plunging into it, however, you should read the author's foreword on the opposite page.

A story of Prince Menes and Sexton Blake
Mysticism —Adventure —Thrills!

Prince Menes and Sexton Blake
An excerpt from an early 'Collector's Digest' monograph.
"Prince Menes, never measured anywhere up to the splendid characterisation of Prince Wu Ling. He ran to only six stories in the "U.J." —four between 722 and 731 then a long gap until 1067 and 1112/13.

G. H. TEED'S work in **"THE UNION JACK"**
No.
722   The Case of Re-Incarnation. Prince Menes.
723   **The Secret Hand**.   Prince Menes.
728   **The Case of the Crimson Terror**. Prince Menes.
731   **The Invisible Ray**.   Prince Menes.
1067   **The Mummy's Twin**.   Prince Menes.
1112   The Adventure of the Blue Bowl.   Yvonne   Cartier & Prince Menes.
1113   The House on the Cliff.   Yvonne Cartier & Prince Menes.

"SEXTON BLAKE LIBRARY"
(Second Series)
19 The Great Canal Plot. Prince Wu Ling, George Marsden Plummer, Prince Menes, The Three Musketeers & The Black Eagle. This was subsequently republished as **Bottom of Suez**, also a Stillwoods Edition.
35 **The Case of the Mummified Hand**. Yvonne   Cartier, Dr. Huxton Rymer, Mary Trent, George Marsden Plummer, Prince Wu Ling, Prince Menes, The Three Musketeers & The Black Eagle.

Bold text indicates available through **Stillwoods**.

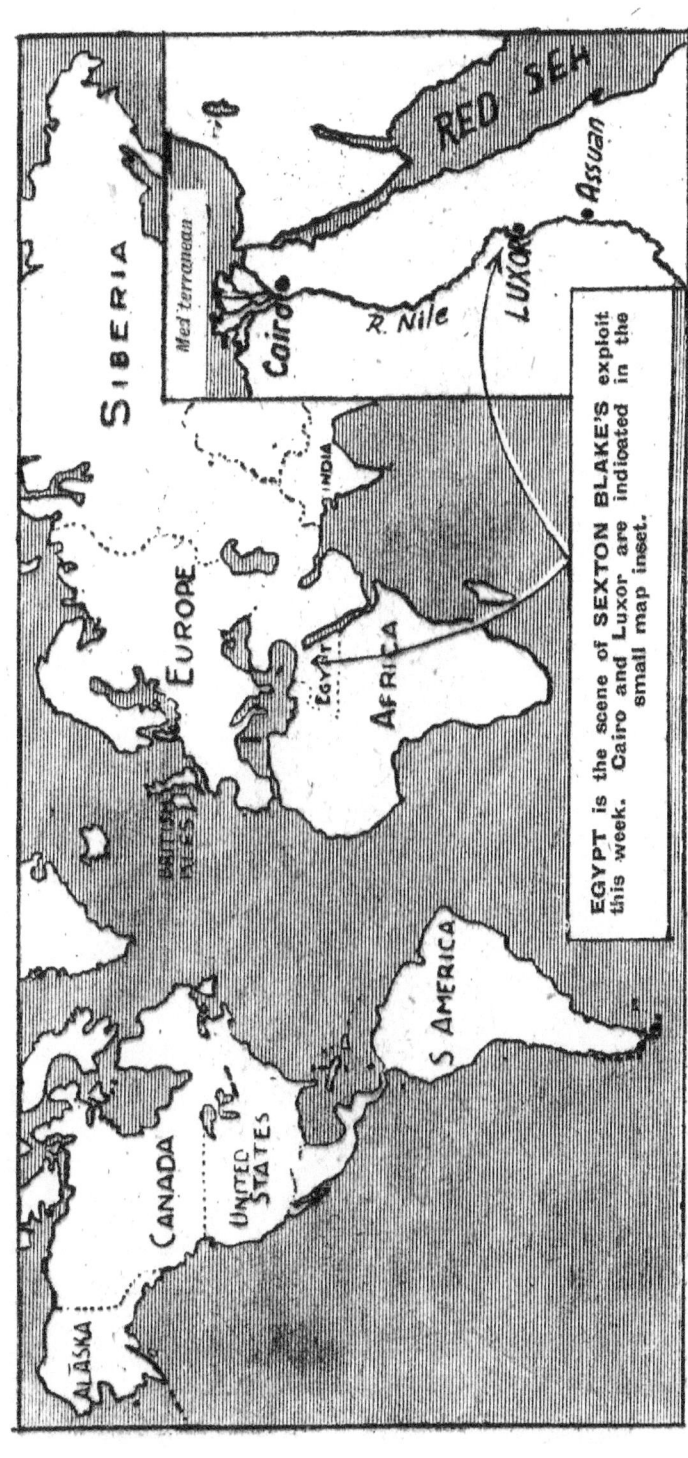

EGYPT is the scene of SEXTON BLAKE'S exploit this week. Cairo and Luxor are indicated in the small map inset.

AUTHOR'S FOREWORD to the Introduction of PRINCE MENES.

AUTHOR'S FOREWORD to the Introduction of PRINCE MENES.

OLD readers of the **UNION JACK** will doubtless recall the stories which appeared in this journal a few years ago under the general series title of "The Vengeance of Ra," and which were comprised under the sub-titles of "The Man from Everywhere," "The Secret Hand," "The Crimson Terror," "The Invisible Ray," etc.

For the benefit of new readers, however, it will be as well to give a brief review of the life, training, and character of that strange individual known as Prince Menes, the Man from Everywhere, supreme head of the ancient Order of Ra, which was founded by the earliest of the Pharaohs in Egypt, and which undoubtedly exists in all its ancient purity of ritual and belief at the present time, although its devious workings, are necessarily of the most secret nature.

Unquestionably it is the controlling spirit behind that strange and savage tribe of desert Arabs known as the Senussi, with whom British troops came into contact during the Great War; and there is good ground for supposing also that the powerful Tut-Ankh-Amen, whose tomb was discovered last year by the late Lord Carnarvon and Mr. Howard Carter, was deeply involved in its activities.

When the reader remembers that the East is still saturated with all the superstitions and strange practices of the past; that many, many things take place there that are never whispered of outside certain circles, and that the belief of Isis and Osiris is still as strong in Egypt beneath the crust, so to say, as it ever was, it will not be difficult to understand why such a strange human product as Prince Menes could be evolved even to-day. Also, it can be understood that the beliefs and practices which inspired him were as potent as they had been ten thousand years ago, when they had guided the first head of the Order of Ra, and whose re-incarnation Prince Menes was believed to be.

In our land we may scoff at the theory of re-incarnation if we will, but after some years in the East the author feels no inclination to do so. There are too many uncanny things there to inspire any such levity of mind when one has once peered beyond the fringe.

At the time Prince Menes first made his sinister force felt in Europe he was just thirty-five years of age. Up to that time his whole life had been entirely a form of intensive training for the work to which his life was to be devoted. Born of a strange union—his father was a Russian duke and his mother a Chinese princess —he very early in life imbibed all the lore which two deeply cultured persons of two strange races could teach him. At the age of ten he wrote, read, and spoke Russian and Chinese fluently, and could have passed a senior test in the literature and history of both peoples.

At the age of ten he was taken from the grand duke's big palace in the Crimea and given into the care of a priest of the Greek orthodox church. This priest had already secretly become a member of a strange Egyptian order known as the Order of Ra, and through certain studies he had made he was convinced that young Menes was the actual re-incarnation of the Prince Menes who had been the founder and first head of the order.

As soon as the child came into his possession he fled with him to the Egyptian desert, where he was at once taken under the protection of the order. There he set himself to educate the boy along certain specified lines, and for the next fourteen years he devoted his every moment to this purpose. Being of a more than ordinarily intelligent nature, Menes proved an apt pupil, and by the time he reached the age of twenty-four he was deeply versed not only in the history of the Order of Ra and all its secret practices, but also in most modern languages and the literature and arts of every country that had left any mark on history.

The next step was travel, and, on leaving Egypt, he and his tutor visited practically every spot on the globe, thus rounding off by direct contact with men and things the mind-training Menes had received.

For six years they travelled constantly, and, on returning to Egypt, Prince Menes was again sent into the desert, where he has been an active novitiate of the Order of Ra.

He spent four years in deep seclusion with the inner circle of priests of the order, and, after passing through every step of each degree, was finally chosen as the supreme head of the order, and hailed as the direct re-incarnation of the first Prince Menes who had founded the brotherhood ten thousand years before, and also as the spiritual re-incarnation of the god Isis who, prophecy said, would dwell in the bodily temple of the incarnated Menes.

By that time the direction of the activities of the order was placed in his sole care; and, since prophecy said that somewhere in the world the spirit of the goddess, Osiris must also be dwelling in the bodily temple of the re-incarnated Queen of Isis, the prince resolved to search until he had found her.

But first he resolved to embark on a campaign of vengeance, which was the result of things that had happened ten thousand years before.

At that time the first Prince Menes was a twin-brother of the ruling Pharaoh, and there had been bitter strife between the two brothers, for the Pharaoh himself had wanted to be the head of the order as well as the ruler of Upper and Lower Egypt.

But the priests had decided against him, and Menes had been chosen. The Pharaoh had intrigued for his brother's downfall, and, through the machinations of ten nobles, Menes had been betrayed, and had been seized and imprisoned in a rock tomb.

He had lived there for sixty years, and just before he died had issued a prophecy which was still believed by the present-day members of the order. This prophecy was to the effect that when ten thousand years had parsed, Menes, the Pharaoh, and the ten guilty nobles would all be re-incarnated on earth at the same time.

While it was, of course, believed that each one would be re-incarnated many times during that long stretch of time, it would be ten thousand years before they would all walk on the earth again at the same time.

And now, with the coming of Prince Menes, it was firmly believed that somewhere out in the world, in some human guise, were the ten nobles who had betrayed him centuries before, and it was Menes' first purpose to seek them out and exact vengeance for his betrayal. As for the Pharaoh who had been his twin-brother, he knew that their spirits would only rest tranquil when they had forgiven each other, and had become reunited in the circle of the Order of Ra.

With that accomplished, it was his purpose to seek out the woman in whose body dwelt the spirit of Osiris, and when he had succeeded in that he believed that a new golden age would dawn for Egypt.

Let it not be thought that this day is not looked for by the Egyptians. It is as much a part of their creed as is the belief of the Jews that eventually their race will fulfil the old Biblical prophecy and return to Judea to found a new kingdom of the Jews. And the unrest of recent years in Egypt is nothing more or less than the seething intrigue underneath forcing itself to the surface.

Whether we believe the present-day Egyptians to be capable of building up a nation is another matter. But they believe it, and it is that belief which has kept alive the secret Order of Ra for ten thousand years —the oldest secret society in the world, and as pure in its ritual to-day as it was in the beginning.

Such is Prince Menes. He is a composite of many members of that order, and his activities, while strange and sinister at times, were entirely within the range of human power, which, when controlled by an ascetic adept of the East, can be made to perform things quite beyond the power of the West to understand —as our own scientists to-day are the first to acknowledge. —THE AUTHOR.

Perhaps there is somebody somewhere who will not care for this story. If so, that person has a very pernickety taste. To those to whom the mysticism of Egypt's past appeals, or the scope of its adventure in the present, this yarn will have irresistible charm. Before plunging into it, however, you should read the author's foreword on the opposite page.

Suddenly the professor became aware that a horseman had appeared close to him. For perhaps a minute the two remained gazing at each other, motionless. Then the mounted man raised his arm, pointing towards the north, and abruptly whirled his horse and went flying across the desert. *(Chapter 1.)*

The First Chapter. The Desert Apparition.

NIGHT —an Egyptian night —heavy, dark, sinister.

The mud-laden Nile was creeping sluggishly along like some evil thing born of the mysterious desert. A spell of silence seemed to hold that land of the ages in a brooding spell. Not a palm-leaf stirred; even the bats and the flying-foxes and nightjars appeared to have departed. Not a single light of man showed along that particular dreary stretch of river.

It was as if all the secret forces of Egypt's amazing past had annihilated every living thing.

Breathless, lifeless it seemed. But in the very heart of the brooding land, in a small portable wooden hut which had been erected close to the bank of the river a few miles above Luxor, three men were seated about a table,

They were not Egyptians of the present; they were not blood descendants of the Egyptians of the past. They were Europeans, of the virile race known from one side of the globe to the other as British.

Three of them there were —an Englishman, a Scotsman, and an Irishman, and those three, had been drawn together by the whim of Fate in that lonely hut on the banks of the Nile in a common effort to probe a little way into the mysterious past of that dark land.

John Rumford, the Englishman, was an amateur antiquarian and the financial force of the party. Lawrence Malone, the Irishman, was the well-known explorer and big-game hunter who would have been a tower of strength on any expedition. James McKenzie, the Scotsman, was small and dried up physically, but as a scientist, a mathematician, and an Egyptologist, his name was one to conjure with in any circle of learned men; and though he rarely did so, he could, if he wished, write a good round dozen of letters after his name.

About two hundred yards away from the hut, as motionless as the sand hollows in which they lay, were a score of blanketed fellaheen who composed the preliminary working gang of the expedition. Beyond was a gloomy-looking structure of wood that held the tools and supplies. This structure, like the small hut, was of the knock down type. Farther on, but invisible in that gloom, was a wild region of stone and sand dunes, which was the subject of the conversation taking place between the three men, and which had been under every mathematical test that Professor McKenzie could apply to it.

For years James McKenzie had given that wonderful mind of his to Egypt and the mysteries of the ancient races, whose mathematical knowledge was almost entirely expressed by examples in stone to which the key was lost long ago, but which undoubtedly comprised more marvels of mathematics and astronomy than we to-day even dream of.

Not only that wild pile near which the hut had been erected had James McKenzie studied. On the contrary, he had patiently examined every known ruin in the whole land, and not the least of his attention had been given to the Great Pyramid and its two smaller satellites outside Cairo, as well as the changeless Sphinx that sits brooding over the barren desert, which once was a land flowing with milk and honey.

He could have told one quite a few things about that little-explored pile, the Great Pyramid, which were unknown even to the guides.

For instance, he could have explained, had he desired, that the Great Pyramid of Gizeh is the only great erection of man which is oriented absolutely to the four points of the compass. Its measurements, if extended, would give the exact weight of the globe in tons, and the mean distance between the earth and the sun in English miles. (From what strange source did our English measurements really come?) Its base is an exact fraction of the diameter of the earth from pole to pole —exactly one ten-millionth part of the earth's semi-axis.

He could have added that it is built within a few feet of the exact centre of the earth's habitable area, and that infinitesimal discrepancy can probably be explained owing to a minute change in the globe in the four thousand odd years that have passed since it was built, or, more likely, since the rock on which it rests was necessary for its foundations.

He could have told you, too, that the descending passage discovered by Al Mamoun in 825 A.D. points directly upwards to the Pole Star, or, rather, what was the Pole Star at that time, Alpha Draconis, when it was at its lowest point of culmination. Its inside temperature is exactly the mean between the boiling and freezing points of water at that level. Its dimensions solve the problem of squaring the circle, because a circular line drawn to the Great Pyramid's vertical height shows the actual squaring of the circle, the length of that line being exactly equal to the length of the four sides forming the base, of the pyramid. One of the most curious features about this mysterious pile is that it can be proved to establish the scientific accuracy of the English gallon measure and the English measure of length as opposed to the Continental metric system.

Professor James McKenzie was one of the few so-called "dry-as-dust" scientists who shared the modern belief that the Great Pyramid was never a tomb, but was nothing more or less than a wonderful marvel in granite of all that was known to the priests of ancient Egypt, and, in its almost unbelievable perfection in thousands of different ways, was simply a secret code expression of that knowledge —built to code for all time in such a way that only the initiates of that ancient order of priests could read its meaning.

And it is a fact that as earnest students get a little deeper beneath the surface of the mystery, they come upon signs of such scientific marvels of mathematical perfection that it is genuinely doubted whether we at present are capable of understanding them.

There is something about that departed race of old Egypt that is uncanny—something that makes one think at times that they must have arrived out of space from Mars or Venus, bringing with them all that untold generations on another planet had known, and that, after expressing this knowledge in that gigantic marvel of stone, had departed whence they came.

One can almost regard them as the advance guard of an invasion to come from one of those distant globes —an invasion that may have its second phase in our time, or may be delayed for another five thousand years, for surely centuries, or even a millenium, loom as but a fleeting moment in the mysterious scheme of the cosmos of which we, on this tiny speck of matter in space, are such an insignificant part.

These facts will serve to give one some idea of the scientific attainments of the technical member of the small expedition the three principals of which were seated in that wooden hut while the black Egyptian night hung heavy over the desert.

There had been nothing haphazard about the preliminary work of the expedition. With unlimited funds provided by John Rumford, with the long experience of James McKenzie to guide them, and the efficient control of the actual work which Lawrence Malone supplied, there would seem to be nothing lacking to make the whole thing a success.

Nor was there. For two years now they had toiled patiently, seeking among those tumbled masses of stone and broken monuments for the location of what Professor McKenzie believed to be the oldest of the tombs of all the Pharaohs.

Not long before, the tomb of a later Pharaoh, Tut-Ankh-Amen, had been discovered in the Valley of the Kings, near Luxor, by the late Lord Carnarvon and his assistant, Mr. Howard Carter. The world had been spellbound with interest as the reports of this wonderful find were given out, but, if Professor McKenzie's calculations were correct, this little expedition, working entirely outside the range of journalistic publicity, was on the verge of making a discovery that would throw the other completely in the shade.

From, certain very complicated calculations he had made, the professor maintained that somewhere in that tumbled heap of ruins, near which they had set their camp, would be found a very much earlier burial-ground than the Valley of the Kings some miles away.

In fact, he even went so far as to insist that it was nothing more or less than the very first of the royal burial-grounds of Egypt, and that he had reason to believe that they would find the tomb and money and treasure of the powerful Pharaoh, Menetakhnan, who was the first Egyptian king to bring Upper and Lower Egypt under one throne.

Fabulous legends have been told of this early king, and if only a part of them are true, then the wealth which was buried with him must have totaled a sum that would cause all the treasures of Tut-Ankh-Amen to pale into insignificance.

And, if the professor's calculations were correct, those three men knew as they sat about that plain deal table that they were on the verge of making the most startling discovery in history.

Under the direction of Lawrence Malone, the whole vast pile of ruins had been minutely surveyed and measured. Somewhere in that extraordinary brain of his, Professor McKenzie had figured out what he claimed would solve the problem, and that solution had been based on nothing more or less than certain mathematical symbols which, he claimed, existed in the measurements of the Great Pyramid of Gizeh.

That pyramid had been built thousands of years after the death of Menetakhnan, but the professor insisted that the science of the ancient priests had been brought to perfection long before that marvel in stone had been erected, and that it but expressed the sum total of knowledge possessed by the old priests.

He even went farther, and claimed that somewhere in Egypt there existed to this day an order which had been maintained in all its purity of ritual from those distant days, and that one day some daring scientist would strike the secret. Should that day ever come, the professor predicted that the world would stand aghast at the amazing things which would be revealed.

John Rumford, millionaire and practical business man, didn't give much thought to this. He had every confidence in Professor McKenzie, and if they could uncover something as fine as King Tut-Ankh-Amen's tomb at Luxor, then he would be perfectly satisfied. As for Lawrence Malone, uncovering old tombs was all in the day's work with him, and all his time was given to the prosecution of the actual survey work,

"To-morrow I can tell you definitely whether we are on a false trail or not," the big, rugged Irishman was saying as he chewed on the end of his pipe. "And it's my opinion that we are on the right track. If so, I shall have the entrance to the tomb uncovered by midday, and then it's up to you, professor. If we do hit the tomb on the present slope, then my hat goes off to you. How you ever managed to figure out that certain measurements of the Great Pyramid at Gizeh would reveal the exact location of Menetakhnan's tomb beats me, but, by ginger, it looks to me as if you were right!"

The little professor's eyes blinked behind his glasses.

"I will show you more than that before we are finished," he said, with a smile. "You are a doubter, Malone. But you need feel no uncertainty. I tell you that you will find the entrance to Menetakhnan's tomb at the bottom of the slope where you are working now. It may not be the inner and secret chamber for which we seek.

"In fact, I shouldn't be very much surprised if we find nothing more than an empty chamber lined with porphyry sheets. From what I have been able to learn of that wily old Pharaoh, he was quite capable of going to extraordinary lengths to ensure that his wealth would not be disturbed after he was once sealed up. But have patience; we shall find the inner hoard eventually!"

"I'm banking, on the professor," rumbled the millionaire. "He hasn't made a false calculation yet, and my banking account stays behind this until he says the word to stop. I am not a very imaginative person, my friends, but I don't mind confessing that to-night I feel as if we were on the verge of big things —queer things. They say some queer things happened last year when the secret of Tut-Ankh-Amen's resting-place was brought to light, and we may strike something of the same sort here."

The professor half rose, then sat down. He drew out his cigarette-case, and selected a thin, yellow cigarette. He lit it carefully, and then blinked, first at Rumford, then at Malone.

"I haven't told you the half of Menetakhnan," he said slowly. "I didn't think it would be wise —at first. But tonight I think the time has come to tell you a little more about him. It will explain why I am convinced that when we do find his inner tomb, we shall find a far greater store of wealth than has ever been brought to light. Would you care to hear it?"

The other two nodded vigorously, and bent over the table to listen. They were interested, for they knew that when the little professor did talk, he was worth listening to.

"I have explained to you that Menetakhnan was the first of the really powerful Pharaohs," he said quietly. "He was more than that. He was a miser on a gigantic scale. He ruled in Upper and Lower Egypt for nearly seventy years, and throughout all that time it seems that he kept his subjects toiling constantly to pile up wealth for him. That he hid most of it seems certain, for there are authentic records still existing in certain hieroglyphics which go to show that for a century after his death Egypt was almost bankrupt.

"But that is by no means the chief point of interest about his reign. He came to the throne as a boy of ten years of age, and it appears that he was chosen by the priestly order instead of his twin brother, Prince Menes, who, on the other hand, was made the supreme head of the priestly order of Ra. Not much is known about what occurred immediately after that, but it seems fairly reasonable to suppose that Menetakhnan grew jealous of his brother, for, of course, when it came down to brass tacks, the priests ruled the throne, and Menes was therefore more powerful than the Pharaoh himself.

"How the king managed things we don't know, but I have deciphered certain glyphs which convince me that Menes was betrayed and kept imprisoned by the Pharaoh for a great many years. Now it was at that point in my investigations that I came upon a most interesting thing. It was a distinct reference to the priestly order of the time, and contained a prophecy which Prince Menes was supposed to have made before dying in prison.

"This was to the effect that ten thousand years would pass before he and his twin brother, and those who had betrayed him, would all again be reincarnated at the same time on earth; that Menes would again be at the head of the Order of Ra, and that, through him, Egypt would once more regain her glory. He seemed to have foreseen that she would fall into decay, as we know she did.

"Well, gentlemen, that prophecy was made many thousands of years ago, and it was a long time after that the Great Pyramid of Gizeh was built. Nevertheless, I, myself, have found certain cryptic references in the great pyramid to that same prophecy, and it is rather interesting to reflect that by my calculations the present month marks a date just ten thousand years after the supposed death of Prince Menes in his prison."

The professor paused, but neither of his listeners attempted to speak. They were too absorbed in the amazing details he was confiding to them. Presently he went on:

"Yes, ten thousand years, this very month. And if there is any truth in the theory of reincarnation, if, by some strange chance, that prophecy of Prince Menes should have been really inspired, then we have to contemplate the stupendous fact, gentlemen, that there are walking the earth to-day the same men who lived when that pile of stone ruins yonder was of virgin newness."

"Pshaw! I don't believe in reincarnation," broke in Malone.

The professor shrugged.

"There may be nothing in it," he conceded. "Still, if is interesting to reflect on the prophecy just the same. Ever since the passing away of the so-called golden age of Egypt she has been nothing more than a desert at the mercy of any stronger power which desired to occupy her. We British have been here for some time, and shall probably continue to control the country as long as the Suez Canal is vital to us. Nevertheless, it is only very recently that we have given her a measure of independence and have created a king. Isn't that the first step towards a rejuvenated Egypt just as the prophecy foretold? Isn't it strange that these changes should begin exactly ten thousand years later, just as Prince Menes foretold?"

"I'll grant you that," said Rumford. "And if this bird Menes is back on the job, then he may want to take a whack at that buried wealth himself. If he has any idea of playing the king game, it would come in mighty useful to him to have a treasury like that to start with,"

Lawrence Malone smiled, but the little professor showed no levity.

"If he could gain a conscious knowledge of what happened in the past, then he would certainly try for the treasure," he said gravely. "And there have been one or two strange occurrences lately, my friends, that make me feel somehow that we are not going to complete our work without encountering obstacles. What those obstacles will be I don't know, but I —"

"My heavens! What was that?"

Both Rumford and Malone uttered the words simultaneously as they came to their feet, their eyes wide with puzzled amaze. From somewhere outside there had suddenly broken out a weird haunting scream that seemed to rise from the very heart of the pile of ruins, and to lift in terrifying cadence through that black and evil night. It was like nothing any one of the three had ever heard before. Malone thought instinctively of the wail of the banshee, but that was as nothing to the inhuman cry which had shattered the night —a sound that seemed laden with terrible evil from the depths of some nameless pit.

All three acted as one man. They swung towards the door and dashed outside. As they got clear of the hut their eyes went instinctively towards the spot where the pile of ruins lay, and each man stood rooted in his tracks at what he saw.

No longer was the night a curtain of black. Over the pile of stone where the professor insisted the tomb of Menetakhnan would be found could be seen a great globe of flame, like nothing more than a gigantic will o' the wisp. Where it had come from none could tell, but as they watched it they saw it begin to rise and drift slowly towards them. Their immediate surroundings were as light as at hot noon. Between them and the ruins they could see the prone forms of the fellahs where they lay like dead men.

Not one of those three Europeans had the faintest streak of cowardice in him, but for all that they drew a little closer together as the globe came nearer and nearer.

Then suddenly it was riven into a million shooting flames, as it exploded with terrific force. The three watchers were hurled to the ground by the concussion, but, strange to say, even though the flames seemed to pass directly over them, they felt no heat!

Half-stunned, they lay as they were for a few seconds, then, as they picked themselves up, the darkness, which had again fallen, was pierced by a strange violet light that appeared to rise from the ground in a wide circle enclosing the ruins, near the edge of which the hut stood.

It rose, and rose higher and higher, expanding upwards like a swelling band until they could see that it was drawing in towards the centre overhead, forming a sort of miniature sky bowl over them as it were. The light grew more intense each moment, until it became almost blinding, and still not an atom of heat reached them.

Lawrence Malone was trying to regard the phenomena as some sudden natural outbreak, due to extraordinary atmospheric conditions. John Rumford was standing at bay, as if he expected each moment to be attacked by some unknown force. The little professor had drawn back a short distance, and was trying to find some scientific explanation for it all.

Thus they stood while that violet light drew closer above them, forming a tiny world all of its own, and then, just as the last vent above them closed, there came another terrific explosion.

Unaware how close he had stepped to the edge of the Nile, Professor McKenzie had instinctively thrown himself down as the second explosion came. But, instead of finding himself down on the ground, he went shooting clean over the edge of the bank, and, a second later, found himself struggling in the sluggish current of the river.

On the bank darkness, heavy and impenetrable, had fallen over everything, and, as he struck out to try and find a landing, he heard once more that strange eerie wail that had sounded before the coming of the phenomena.

He had no idea what had happened to Malone and Rumford. Whether they had been stunned by the second explosion he could not tell. They might have been hurled into the river, as he had been. It was impossible to guess, and to his repeated cries no answer came.

It was more than half an hour before he succeeded in making a landing, and, as far as he could make a guess, he figured he must be some two or three miles at least below the camp. It would be impossible for him to make his way back through the darkness. All he could do was to wait until the first streaks of dawn should come to guide him.

He sat shivering on the river-bank during hours that seemed like eternity, and as the first grey showed over the desert to the east, he rose and began walking stiffly along the bank. He found his guess was a good one, for he reckoned he had covered between two and three miles when at last he reached the camp —or, rather, when he reached the spot where the camp had been, for of the hut there was not a single trace left. It had disappeared as if some giant hand had plucked it bodily from the spot, and carried it into the desert.

Not was there any sign of Malone and Rumford. They, too, had disappeared, and a few moments showed the professor that every one of the fellahs was gone, too. Not a shred of the storage shack was to be seen —not a single tool, not one rag to show that the camp of an expedition had been there the previous night.

The heap of tumbled ruins was still there, however, and, completely at a loss to understand the meaning of it all, the professor walked towards it. He found the sloping tunnel which Malone had driven towards the tomb of the Pharaoh, but not a man or tool was to be seen. The professor turned away, and was standing gazing thoughtfully towards the desert, when suddenly he became aware that a horseman had suddenly appeared close to him. He turned, and found himself gazing into the dark eyes of a hooded figure in white who was sitting relaxed in the saddle, gazing at him strangely.

For perhaps the space of a minute the two remained motionless. Then the mounted man raised his arm and pointed towards the north with an imperative gesture. With that the horseman whirled suddenly, and went flying across the desert, leaving the professor more mystified than ever.

MR. SEXTON BLAKE had never personally met Professor James McKenzie, the eminent Egyptologist, but he was a member of the same scientific body to which the professor belonged, and thus received all the private bulletins published by that society.

In this way he had closely followed the work of exploration in which the professor had been engaged for some time past, and when Mrs. Bardell appeared one morning, bearing a small tray on which reposed Professor McKenzie's card, Blake gave instructions that he was to be shown up at once.

He greeted his visitor with considerable deference, for he had a very deep respect for his scholarly attainments, but it was soon evident that the professor had not come for any idle purpose.

"I reached England yesterday, Mr. Blake," he said, when he was seated. "I have come through from Egypt for the special purpose of consulting you. I know that you have considerable knowledge of Egyptian politics, and conditions in general there, and while I, too, have made some study of the country, I regret that it has been confined almost entirely to the things concerning the ancient days. To be brief, I have come to England to consult you professionally."

Blake smiled.

"I hardly think I can give much advice to a man with your knowledge of Egypt, professor," he said. "I know the country well; and I have been a student of Egyptology in so far as my profession has permitted, but your own investigations there are far, far beyond anything I have reached."

"Tut, Mr. Blake! I don't know anything about modern Egypt. And that is just why I decided to come to you. About the past —well, we will say that I have scratched the surface, and let it go at that. But my immediate problem is one of the present, and it is serious."

"I am concerned to hear that. Has it something to do with your recent work there?"

"Yes. Do you know Lawrence Malone?"

"The explorer? Yes; quite well!"

"Ever meet John Rumford? He has been financing our work out there."

"I have never met him; but, of course, I know the name quite well."

"Good! Well, they have been with me out there. To make as clear as I can just what has happened, I had better give you a brief outline of the work we have been engaged upon."

"I have kept in touch with your reports to the society, professor. I have the last pamphlet which, I believe, covers your work up to some three months ago."

"That will save time. You know, then, that we have been trying to locate the tomb of one of the earliest Pharaohs —Menetakhnan?"

"Oh, yes!"

"You will know from the pamphlets which the society has issued that I consider it of far more importance to locate Menetakhnan's tomb than that of Tut-Ankh-Amen, which has been successfully accomplished, and about which there has been considerable publicity.

"That was a wonderful achievement, but we have been after a far richer prize, and, although we have managed to work out of the glare of publicity, I can tell you in confidence that we have actually located the tomb we have been seeking. So far, every one of my calculations have been proved correct.

"In fact, about two weeks ago, Malone, who had charge of the actual work of excavation, had almost entirely cleared the descending passage to the tomb, and we were on the eve of uncovering the outer door of the place, when a most bewildering and incomprehensible occurrence took place. It is that which has brought me to England to see you. I will explain.

"We located the tomb among a vast heap of old ruins some miles above Luxor. These, ruins I had always maintained were far older than those in the Valley of the Kings, and were, in my opinion, the scene of the very earliest of the royal burial-grounds of Egypt. The result of our work already shows that my view was correct.

"It has taken us two years to find the tomb we sought, but this season, as I have said, we succeeded, We had a more or less permanent camp there, where Malone, Rumford, and myself lived, together with the gang of native labourers who were working under Malone.

"That was the situation up to the eve of the day on which we intended uncovering Menetakhnan's tomb. On that night —it was a typical heavy, black Egyptian night —we were seated in our hut, arranging the last details before starting with the work on the morrow, when a phenomena occurred —the strangest thing I have ever experienced.

"It was, as near as may be, half an hour after midnight when we were startled to hear an uncanny wailing sound outside the hut. All three of us rushed out, and off to one side we observed, just above the pile of ruins where we had located the tomb, a large globe of what appeared to be pure flame.

"I have seen marsh gas, and once I witnessed a small ball of flame which appeared at a certain place in India just after a thunderstorm. This globe of fire was something like that, if you follow what I mean, but larger —very much larger. I should say in size it was equal to an ordinary observation balloon.

"Well, Mr. Blake, we were held spellbound, thinking that we were witnessing some strange atmospheric phenomenon, and, while we stood gazing at it, the globe exploded with a terrific report. The shock of the explosion threw us to the ground, but I was not seriously injured, and I do not believe that my two companions suffered, either. Following that we were amazed to see a deep band of a peculiar violet light rise from the ground, as it were, and begin to widen and narrow above like an inverted bowl of flame.

"It is difficult for me to describe just what it was like, but as I watched it I saw that it was drawing closer and closer in at the top. It seemed to encircle the whole camp, including the heap of ruins, and I can recall thinking that if it did close entirely at the top it would seem like a miniature world of our own —a tent of light over us and our camp.

"Well, sir, that is exactly what happened. And on the very instant that the vent at the top closed there came another terrific explosion. Just what happened then I do not know. For myself, I was thrown into the Nile —I had been standing close to the edge of the bank. I found myself struggling in the water, and, although the current is sluggish there, it took me a good half-hour to find a spot where I could land, owing to the steepness of the bank.

"I could see no signs of any huts, and as the country thereabouts is very wild, I dared not risk trying to make my way along in the dark. I sat on the bank until morning; then, as soon as dawn began to show, I walked back to the camp.

"I say the camp; but when I arrived there I found that what had been the camp had entirely disappeared. The knock-down hut which Malone, Rumford, and I had used had completely vanished, as had the larger shack where the tools and supplies had been stored.

"But that was by no means all. Of Malone and Rumford there wasn't a sign, and the thirty-odd labourers were nowhere to be seen. Of course, it is possible that the phenomena may have filled them with such fright that they bolted in a body into the desert; but Malone and Rumford would do nothing of the sort."

"I can't imagine Malone doing so," remarked Blake.

"Nor Rumford. Well, to make the story as short as possible, Mr. Blake, I searched all about the place, but came upon nothing. The pile of ruins was still there. The excavated passage was just as it had been the day before. But nothing else —not a shred or a scratch of the camp was to be seen.

"There was something uncanny about it that got under my skin. I was determined, however, to solve the mystery if possible; and, after a general survey of the ground, I set to work in the descending passage which had been dug under Malone's direction.

"It was while I was poking about there that I suddenly became aware that I was not alone. I glanced up, to see a native horseman close to me. I didn't hear or see him come, but he was there right enough. He was sitting his horse, gazing at me in a most strange manner. At first I was too surprised to speak, and before I could frame a sentence he had made an imperative gesture as if to warn me away from the spot, and an instant after he and his horse had dashed off towards the desert.

"Well, sir, I spent a couple of days about the place, and then I was forced to go down to Luxor as I had an attack of fever. As soon as I was well again I renewed my efforts to find out what had become of Malone and Rumford, but I was unable —have been unable —to find a single trace of them. From the moment that second explosion took place they have disappeared as completely as if they had evaporated into the atmosphere. I have combed the whole of Egypt, but not a sign have I found."

"Do you mean that to this day you have heard nothing from them?"

"Not a word."

"And the labourers?"

"Just the same. Not a sign of one of them."

"Were there any signs that the hut and the store shack had been consumed by fire?"

"No. I looked for marks of the sort, but there was nothing. Besides, even if the buildings had been burned, the metal parts of the tools would have been left."

"Um! That is true. It seems to have been a very strange occurrence, professor."

"It would have to be to bring me back to England so suddenly. I have tried to find some natural explanation, but cannot do so. I am convinced that there is some devilfish hanky-panky behind it all, and that is why I have come to you."

"You mean some subtle human agency?"

"Exactly!"

"Have you any suspicions?"

"Nothing definite, but —I —" And the professor hesitated. Then he said: "I will tell you something that may sound fantastic to you, Mr. Blake. It is a thing I would speak of to very few men, for most persons would be inclined to scoff at it. As a matter of fact, I was engaged in speaking of this very thing to Malone and Rumford when the phenomena occurred. To your analytical mind the whole thing may sound grotesque. I will confess that it did to me at first. But since then I have seen and heard many things, and now I don't know —I don't know!"

"If this thing of which you speak is sufficiently important for your scientific mind to take into consideration, I do not think you will find me a scoffer, professor," said Blake quietly. "Please tell me about it, by all means."

Then Professor McKenzie began, and related to Sexton Blake the sum and substance of what he had been telling Lawrence Malone and John Rumford when the strange occurrence above Luxor had interrupted his narrative and had apparently swept his two companions as well as the gang of labourers completely out of existence.

Sexton Blake listened in silence. He did not move or speak until his visitor had come to the very end of his tale. Then he said:

"There was no danger of my scoffing at that, professor. In fact, I think I am going to surprise you now. You speak of a man called Menes —Prince Menes. I am inclined to suspect that the silent-horseman whom you saw while searching for Malone and Rumford was none other than he."

"Menes! What makes you think that, Mr. Blake?"

Blake rose, and, with a slight gesture, excusing himself, walked across to the bookcase containing the volumes of the famous "Index." Opening the glass door, he ran his finger along the backs of several volumes until he came to the one he sought. He drew this out and carried it back to his desk. There he opened it and searched among the pages. Then:

"Listen, Professor McKenzie! I will read you what I have relating to the man known as Prince Menes. It is some years now since I have heard anything about him. I did not know whether he had retired to some desert monastery, or whether he was working behind the scenes in recent Egyptian agitation.

"But a few years ago that man was in this country. He was guilty of several crimes, not excepting murder. What you tell me about the early Pharaoh, Menetakhnan, being his twin brother, and existing at the time of the first Prince Menes, is new to me, but I already know that the present Prince Menes claims to be the reincarnated Menes who was the first head of the mysterious Order of Ra, which was conceived by the priests at that time.

"Through various sources I learned something of his early life and a little of the present-day Order of Ra, I suppose, including you and myself, not half a dozen men of this country suspect or believe in the existence of such an order. But, myself, I am convinced that it does exist, and that it functions far more widely than even we suspect."

"You interest me profoundly, Mr. Blake. I am most anxious to hear what you know about this man."

Blake drew the volume of the "Index" towards him. Beginning at the first entry Tinker had been able to make at the time the mysterious Prince Menes had swum into their ken, he read extract after extract to the amazed professor, which covered practically the same ground as that covered by the introductory note to this record.

It was a strange story as told in Blake's level tones that morning in the prosaic consulting-room at Baker Street. It was a tale dealing with fantastic intrigue of a dead race. It was the tale of a mighty people now gone to dust.

It was the exposition of a belief that has existed for more than ten thousand years among certain races, and which, no matter what the Westerner may think of it, has unquestionably produced some extraordinary things.

Alongside this there were annotations touching on the matter-of-fact present— records of the cold, mathematical analyses made in that same consulting-room when Menes had first come to England, and Sexton Blake had tackled his first case of that series which Tinker, with a somewhat romantic touch, had classified in the "Index" under the record title of the "Vengeance of Rah."

When Blake had finished he pushed the book on to the desk.

"Those are the bald facts as jotted down by my assistant," he said. "But I have read sufficient to show you that the man of whom you speak, and he whom I knew as Prince Menes, are one and the same. Therefore, in view of what you have told me of Menetakhnan, I am inclined to agree with you, professor, that phenomena you witnessed on the banks of the Nile was no atmospheric manifestation, nor, in fact, anything supernatural, but, rather, just what you stated — devilish hanky-panky on the part of someone whose motive was to drive you and your party away from the vicinity of Menetakhnan's tomb, to prevent you from making further efforts to enter it."

"I, too, am more than ever convinced such is the case," muttered the little professor. "But do you think —can it be —"

"That Prince Menes is behind it?" interrupted Blake. "I should say on a guess —yes. Don't forget, professor, that he is the present head of an old and most learned order, which has in its possession many, many secrets of science which have been lost to us through the ages. It is true that during the last century our own scientists have made wonderful discoveries in many ways, but we do know that a great deal was known to the ancient priests of Egypt —is probably known to the Order of Ra to-day —which we have been unable to rediscover."

"That is true," admitted the visitor. "But what I want to find out is —what has become of Malone and Rumford, not to mention that gang of poor fellahs?"

"Ah, now you are speaking of something concrete. We cannot even guess what has become of them, any more than we can guess how the hut and the stores shack disappeared so miraculously. I do not believe for a single moment that everything was swept away by that violent light phenomenon of which you have told me. It is possible that the trick was pulled off under cover of that, and I firmly believe that if you had not been precipitated into the Nile you would not be sitting here to-day. It was meant to be a clean sweep, and only that accident prevented it from being so."

"It looks like it. Anyway, it doesn't matter about Menetakhnan now. He can wait. What I want is to find my friends, and I want you to help me to do so, Mr. Blake."

Blake was thoughtful for a few minutes. "I want to ask you a few questions, professor."

"Go ahead. I shall answer to the best of my ability."

"When you finally managed to make a landing that night, you say you sat on the bank of the river until dawn?"

"Yes."

"Then you proceeded back on foot to the scene of the phenomena?"

"Yes."

"You saw or heard no signs of natives during the night?"

"Nothing. If I had seen a light, or heard anything, I should have made for it. The banks of the Nile just there are nothing but sand and rock. It is barren, and there is no cultivation."

"I see. Then I am to take it that the only living person you saw was the strange horseman who acted so queerly?"

"That is correct."

"You say that after a fruitless search at the scene of the phenomena you went down to Luxor?"

"Yes."

"Did you speak to anyone there of the events of that night?"

"I did. I met two of the gentlemen who are preparing Tut-Ankh-Amen's tomb for this season's work, and I mentioned a few things to them. They told me that on the night I referred to, a bright light, low in the sky, had been seen from Luxor, and that it had been put down to a slow-travelling meteor."

"Did you tell them about Malone and Rumford?"

"I didn't tell anyone of their disappearance, but I made inquiries about them. No one had seen them pass through Luxor. You understand, Mr. Blake, the whole thing would sound so fantastic to anyone who had not actually witnessed it that I was a little diffident about speaking of it."

"I can understand that easily enough. Then did you tell no one in Egypt about it?"

"Oh, yes. I went on to Cairo, and took the chief of the British C.I.D. into my confidence. I explained to him just what had occurred;

and, while at first I fancy he thought I was mad, he was at last convinced that something unusual had occurred. He promised to make every possible investigation, and he did so."

"With what result?"

"None whatsoever."

"Um! And it was just after that, I take it, you decided to come to England?"

"Yes, Mr. Blake. I came to the conclusion that the mystery could only be handled by a man who knew modern Egypt through and through. Although I have been deeply absorbed in my own work, I have always taken the time to follow, as far as possible, reports of your cases, and from what I have read I have gathered that you have been mixed up in several recent affairs in Egypt."

"I know a little something of modem Egypt, professor. But exactly what is it you wish me to do?"

"Combine with me in order to uncover the devilry that was afoot that night on the banks of the Nile, and discover, if possible, what has become of Lawrence Malone and John Rumford. Menetakhnan's tomb can wait. My two friends come first. What aid I can give you regarding my knowledge of old Egypt is, of course, at your disposal. But my own belief is that you, with your knowledge of the country as it is to-day —its secret societies, its intrigues, and the political shuffling that is going on beneath the surface —are the one man to tackle the job. Needless to say, Mr. Blake, you may name your own fee."

Blake shrugged.

"I don't need a fee, professor, to try to find my old friend Lawrence Malone. I feel honoured that you believe me capable of handling such a matter. There is only one answer for me to give."

"And that is?"

"Yes, of course!"

"And when could you arrange to start for Egypt, Mr. Blake?" asked the little professor, with a pleased expression in his eyes.

Blake glanced at the silver desk clock. "It is now half-past eleven," he remarked. "There is a train from Victoria for the Continent at half-past four in the afternoon. We could go by that as far as Paris, and then make direct connections for Brindisi. That is the quickest way, and it will enable us to get started up the Nile —if we decide to do that —six days hence. Will that suit you?"

"Decidedly. I am greatly pleased that you will leave this very day. I feared you might need some days to arrange your affairs here."

"I can manage all right. Of course, my assistant accompanies me."

"I leave all the arrangements in your hands, Mr. Blake."

"Very well, professor. Then shall we say four-fifteen at the station —the Continental line?"

"I shall be there."

With that the professor rose and held out his hand.

"I am not going to try and thank you, Mr. Blake." he said, with a little tremble of emotion in his voice. "But I feel deeply grateful for having you take up this matter. I shall bring along everything I have which bears on the matter, and we can go into things on the way."

Blake nodded, and a few seconds later Professor McKenzie took his departure.

And it was just five and a half days later that Blake, Tinker, and the professor were installed at Shepheard's Hotel, in Cairo, where Blake was busy on his plans for the next step in the mystery which faced them.

/drf

SEXTON BLAKE did not deceive himself that anything but the utmost vigilance and the most subtle form of campaign would serve them.

In the modern world in which Prince Menes moved and had his being, Blake's own records were of far greater value than anything the professor knew. The latter had lived for many years in the events of the past, and to him Menes meant the supreme head of the Order of Ra, who had died many thousands of years ago.

As for the ancient prophecy, neither he nor Blake spent much time on that. In the previous cases handled by Blake when he had been up against Prince Menes of the present era, he had come upon many curious things, and he knew as well as the professor that a secret order did still exist in Egypt, and that it was supposed to have flourished without a single break through all those ages.

It was not a question of reincarnation with Blake. Such a thing might or might not be possible. What concerned him was that the present head of the Order of Ra was actively engaged in some secret campaign against the British, and he was willing to acknowledge that it might be pure coincidence that the present Prince Menes was determined that the tomb of the ancient king Menetakhnan should not be opened by anyone but himself.

That Menetakhnan had been the twin brother of the first Prince Menes might or might not hold an academic interest. That could wait. What had to be dealt with immediately was the concrete fact that on the very eve of the unsealing of Menetakhnan's tomb two of the British party engaged on the work had disappeared after the appearance of certain puzzling phenomena.

One thing stood out as a curious point to which Blake gave a good deal of thought. In his conversations with the professor on the way out to Egypt, he discovered that the licence from the Egyptian Government, which had been granted for the expedition, was due to run out inside the next fortnight.

In view of what had occurred on that night of sinister mystery, that fact was significant. If the professor had vanished, as had Malone and Rumford, then there would have been no one left to renew the licence for that particular spot, and the next applicant would have been able to continue his work.

Significant—decidedly so! Therefore, the first thing Blake charged the professor to do on their arrival in Egypt was to take steps to renew the licence. In this certain difficulties arose, and it had been necessary to bring the matter before the British authorities before a renewal was granted.

It was easy enough for Blake to discern Egyptian influence behind this matter, and he was not greatly surprised when the authorities took advantage of their option to make the renewal for only another six months, instead of the original two years.

However, six months was better than nothing, for it gave them the right to occupy the spot for that length of time; and this was exactly what Blake proposed doing.

During the time the professor and Tinker had been busy getting the renewal of the licence, Blake had been spending his days and most of his nights in mysterious absences. Neither of the other two knew what he was up to, nor did they get a hint of it until one evening when they had been in Cairo about a week.

It was just about half-past six when Tinker and the professor went up to their rooms to dress for dinner.

Tinker had just started to take off his whites when the door burst open, and Professor McKenzie appeared. It was evident to the lad that he was in a state of agitation, for his glasses had slipped down on his nose, and his hair was all askew, as if he had been rumpling it while trying to find the explanation of some problem.

"What is it, sir?" asked the lad quickly.

"Tinker, my boy, read this. I found it tucked inside the little velvet box where I keep my evening studs. It is from Mr. Blake, I think —or, at least, it is supposed to be."

Without a word Tinker took the small sheet of paper, and glanced at the close, fine writing.

"No doubt about it, sir," he said. "That is the guv'nor's writing, all right." Then he began to read. This is what had been written on the sheet of thin rice paper:

"I hope you get this safely, professor" (it began). *"It is meant for you and Tinker. By the time you receive it (if you do) I shall be on my way up the Nile. To-morrow morning I want you and Tinker to follow. At nine o' clock you will be visited by the captain of a dahabeah which I have engaged for you. You can trust this man implicitly.*

"On reaching the dahabeah you will find it all ready to start.

Besides the crew there will be a gang of labourers— twenty in all. On board also is a full complement of camp equipment, including tents, tools, and food supplies. I do not think I have missed out a single item, so there will be nothing for you to worry about except any personal things you wish to take along.

"Above all, do not worry if you do not see me for some time. I am following another line, and I want you and Tinker to resume operations on Menetakhnan's tomb as if nothing had happened. If it is necessary I shall find means to communicate with you, but do not betray in the slightest way that you have any knowledge of me. Also, Tinker had better use another name and pose as a young student of Egyptology. That is all until you hear from me again. Don't fail to leave tomorrow morning, as, after that hour, your lives will be in danger. —S. B."

"What do you think of that, my lad?" asked the professor, when Tinker had finished reading.

Tinker handed the letter back to the elder man.

"I think I'd burn that at once, sir," he said. "It is certainly from the guv'nor, and there is nothing else to do but to obey his instructions. I don't know any more than you do what he is up to, or what he has been up to for the past week, but, take it from me, sir, that he has worked out some plan which it is necessary for him to keep to himself for the present. If the captain of the dahabeah turns up to-morrow morning, we must be prepared to leave with him at once."

"I think you are right, Tinker —yes, I think you are right. But I wish I knew what his plan was."

"Don't you worry about that, sir. I'd like to know myself, but the guv'nor will communicate with us when the right moment comes. He never plays a card until he is pretty certain what he is up against."

"Very well, my lad. We shall do as he says. We shall have dinner, and afterwards get our things ready to leave in the morning. Now I wonder how that letter came to be inside my little velvet box?"

Tinker grinned,

"I think it very likely, professor, that it was put there by the guv'nor himself. I shouldn't be at all surprised if he was in the hotel this afternoon. Anyway, he has said nothing about his own luggage, so I shall go along and see if he has taken any of it with him. If not, then I shall lock his room and leave it there until he returns to Cairo."

"Yes, my lad; a good idea. Here is the letter. Perhaps it would be better to burn it, as you suggested."

Tinker took the letter, and, after reading it once more, drew out his match-case, and held it between his fingers until the last vestige of the thin paper had frizzled to an ash. Then he ground the charred fragments between his hands and dropped the grey ashes in the waste-paper-basket.

The professor elected to accompany him along to Blake's room. On entering it, Tinker made a quick survey, which proved that Blake had apparently taken nothing with him except one of his heaviest automatics, which, having duplicate keys to Blake's bags, Tinker discovered missing from one of them. This discovery was followed by another, disclosing the fact that some four hundred rounds of ammunition were also gone. As Tinker closed and locked the bag, he gave a low whistle.

"My sainted aunt!" he muttered. "It looks as if the guv'nor intended starting a little war all on his own!"

They repaired to their rooms then, and when he was dressed, Tinker went down to wait for the professor in the lounge. As their rooms were on the first floor, he did not worry about using the lift, but walked down leisurely, and made his way along to the palm-court, where he ordered an innocuous cocktail. As he settled back in his chair, he suddenly caught sight of a man whom he now recalled having seen several times during the past few days.

The man was an Egyptian, and, although dressed in European clothes, wore the red fez. Tinker had noticed him two or three times when he and the professor were out attending to the renewal of the licence, and on several expeditions of his own into the bazaar, had caught sight of him again.

Up till then he had paid little or no attention to the matter, but now, as he caught the man's steady gaze, he read therein an expression that he did not like. It was not exactly threatening, but it seemed to bore him through and through. After a few moments Tinker seemed to feel an irresistible desire to get up and go across to the man.

He pulled himself together with a jerk and made an effort to turn his eyes casually towards the other end of the room.

"Trying to hypnotise me," he muttered to himself. "I fell for that once at the Central Station in Madras, in India, and I won't be caught napping again. I wonder what the dickens he wants of me? Come to think of it, I've seen him a lot lately. Couldn't have been coincidence, after all, as I thought.

"I wonder. The guv'nor warned us in his letter to watch out, but he said our lives would be in danger after tomorrow. He must have had some notion that we were being watched, and that his own plans might leak out. Anyway, I sha'n't say anything to the professor about this. I'll keep a sharp eye out, for it is possible he may be mixed up with the gang we are after. These birds out here seem to get their information from every point. But if he bothers me he'll stop a bit of lead all right."

At that moment he saw the professor coming towards him, so hastily gulping down the remains of his cocktail, he went to join him. As he did so, he saw the man, who had roused his curiosity, rise, and walk towards the front lounge. When Tinker saw him disappear, he and the professor turned and made their way into the big dining-room, where they were lucky enough to secure a table close to the cooling fountain.

Tinker was somewhat silent during the meal, and so was the professor. Each was mulling over in his own way the letter which had come so mysteriously from Blake, It didn't seem likely that anyone but Blake would be able to put the note just where it had been put, and where a person knowing the professor's habits, knew he must find it that evening. And there was no question of forgery. Tinker knew his master's handwriting too well to be fooled on that point.

As for Tinker, he was wondering just where Blake was at that moment. Blake had given no hint of how he intended to travel into Upper Egypt, whether by river-steamer or by rail. The lad figured it all depended on just how soon he wished to arrive at his destination, which might or might not be the Wadi Abbad, where the professor and his two companions had been excavating in their endeavour to locate Menetakhnan's tomb.

But that Blake had left no detail unattended to was evident from his letter. Every item of equipment had been arranged for, and Tinker knew the country well enough to realise just how difficult it must have been for Blake to secure a dahabeah captain whom he seemed so sure of.

However, he knew he was only wasting grey matter in trying to probe Blake's purpose, so he gave it up and started the professor on his hobby, which was naturally Egyptology.

After dinner, at Tinker's suggestion, they took a tram ride out to Gizeh and back. It was a beautiful moonlight night, and as they walked about almost in the shadow of the Great Pyramid, and gazed at the brooding Sphinx, it was impossible not to feel the dark influence of the mystic past. In those moments anything—anything seemed possible, and from that moment Tinker was not able to shake off the feeling that descended upon him, not until he should once more feel the crisp, salt spume of the Mediterranean whipping across his face.

It was a little after eleven when they got back to the hotel, and as they both had some packing to do in readiness for the morning, they at once proceeded upstairs

Tinker said good-night to the professor at the top of the stairs, and while the latter went down the corridor to the left, Tinker made his way to the right, his and Blake's rooms being in that direction. Before he reached his door Tinker came to a pause, and after a second's hesitation muttered:

"I'll just have a final squint at the guv'nor's room to see that things are all right."

With that he took out the key of Blake's door —which he had thrust in his pocket earlier in the evening —and opened the door. He turned on the light, and then stood on the threshold aghast at what met his eyes.

There could not be the slightest doubt that the room had been entered during his absence, for the luggage was thrown about in great disorder, and the contents had been scattered in every direction.

For the moment Tinker ignored the professor, who had slipped to the floor. He raced after the native and fired a second time. Immediately there came a sharp cry and the sound of something falling heavily to the ground beneath the window.
(*Chapter* 4.)

TINKER closed the door and strode across to the nearest bag. A cursory examination showed that it had been cut just under the lock, and that a thorough inspection of the contents had been made. Every bag had been attacked in the same way, and each had been ruined by the cutting of the leather.

Tinker soon found that nothing of value had been taken away, which was proof enough that those who had entered the room had been in search of some particular object which the lad was positive they had failed to discover.

What the vandals had expected to find was a puzzler to Tinker. If they had only known that Sexton Blake was the last person to leave anything relating to any case on which he might be engaged lying in a bag in his room at an hotel, they had a lot to learn about him.

"A pretty mess!" he muttered. He walked to the windows and ascertained that they were closed and locked, showing that the vandals had come in by the door. "They've had their pains for nothing, I'm willing to bet, but they've made a pretty mess of the guv'nor's things. I'll report this at the office in the morning. I wonder what their object was?"

But the litter on the floor gave no reply. So, after a final glance round, Tinker opened the door, turned off the light, then closed the door and locked it after him. He went quickly along to his own room and thrust in his key. Before turning it, however, he tried the handle, and he was not greatly surprised when it turned easily in his hand, and the door opened under slight pressure. He switched on the light, and, as he stood just inside the door, he saw, to his disgust, that his own luggage had received the same treatment by the vandals. It was lying all about the room, and not a single item had been overlooked.

Tinker closed the door and his jaw set.

"They surely made a good job of it while they were at it," he said aloud. "I hope it kept fine for them while they were at work. A fat lot they would find in my outfit. But it is plain that they are trying to locate some particular thing. I wonder what it is? At any rate, it proves that the guv'nor was right when he warned us to be on guard. If I hadn't been out at Gizeh I'd probably be lying in this heap with a bullet or a knife in my heart.

"But what can it be that they are looking for? I wonder if it can be the letter the guv'nor sent to the professor, if they have got wind of that in some way? It won't be difficult for them to see how the professor and I go, so, the guv'nor must have given them the slip. If that is so, then let them amuse themselves as much as they want to. The hotel will have the other end of the fun by buying a nice lot of travelling-bags."

Then suddenly Tinker gave a start and turned towards the door.

"The professor!" he muttered. "I wonder if they have visited his room, too? By ginger, I'll go along and see!" With that he turned and jerked open his door. As he did so something banged against it, and he knew it was his automatic, which he had placed in his pocket before going out to Gizeh. During the course of their last case in Egypt, both Blake and Tinker had been attacked by a special squad sent from one of the Egyptian secret societies to "get" them, and it had been one of the hottest fights they had had for many years before they finally managed to win through and get back to Cairo. Hence his reason for having his automatic in his pocket that evening.

He ran along the corridor, passed the head of the stairs and the lift-well, and finally reached the door of the professor's room. He paused and rapped sharply. Then he called:

"Professor —professor, are you there?" There, came no answer; but, placing his ear close to the door, Tinker could hear what seemed like a low, moaning sound.

"Something wrong in there." he muttered.

He drew back and surveyed the doors for a moment or two. They were of the long, double French type, and Tinker hadn't any great idea of their strength. He was certain that the professor would have answered him had it been possible to do so, and hence he felt certain there must be someone else in the room.

He made up his mind quickly. Drawing his automatic, he stepped back a couple of paces, then he drove himself forward, his left shoulder braced for the attack on the door.

He hit it with all his force and with the weight of his whole body behind the sturdy, muscular shoulder he sent the doors crashing inwards. As he lurched over the threshold he jerked his pistol up ready for action, and an instant later there was a sharp explosion as he fired at a figure that was just disappearing through the window.

From the end of the bed, where he had apparently been under some form of torture, the professor had slipped to the floor. For the moment Tinker ignored him as he raced after the native who had slipped over the sill. He fired a second time, and immediately there came a sharp cry and the thud of something heavy falling to the ground beneath.

Tinker knew he had made a hit, and as he leant out he was able to distinguish something white lying in a heap on the ground. The next moment two other figures appeared, and with almost unbelievable speed picked up the limp form. They were off at a sharp trot across towards the rear of the hotel, and before they disappeared Tinker took a couple of pot-shots at them. He could not tell if he had made a hit, for the next second they had disappeared behind a clump of bushes, and Tinker knew only too well how useless it would be to follow. Besides, he was anxious about the professor, so he turned back to attend to him.

Professor McKenzie was just getting slowly to his feet. The lad assisted him to a chair, then searched round until he found a flask of brandy. He poured some of the spirit into a glass and pressed a little between the professor's lips. The latter nodded his thanks, and was trying to speak, when the form of a hotel servant appeared between the broken doors.

Before he had a chance to speak —he had evidently been sent to find out the reason for the pistol-shots that had been heard —Tinker lifted his automatic and sprang for the door.

"Get out!" he ordered curtly.

With that he slammed the doors to as well as he could, and then placed a heavy chair against them. That done, he went back to the professor.

"Are you all right, sir?" he asked solicitously.

"Yes, thanks to you, my lad!" answered the professor in a husky voice. "Those brutes —there were two of them —got hold of me the moment I entered my room. I was helpless in their hands, for I am too old to put up any sort of fight. They had apparently been going through my luggage when I came in, as you can see some of the bags have been turned out.

"They placed me over the end rail of the bed, and then asked me what had become of the letter I received this evening. When I refused even to acknowledge that I had received one they began to torture me. That is all, my boy. Before they had gone very far you appeared and drove them off. But it has shaken me."

"You'll be all right by the morning, sir," said Tinker cheerfully. "I winged one of them all right, for he did the high dive from the window-sill into the garden. A couple of his pals dragged him away. The second man you spoke of must have got away."

The professor nodded.

"He did —he made for the window just after you rapped on the door."

"The beastly coward!" muttered Tinker. Then aloud: "Well, sir, I don't think they will return to-night. If they do they will get a warm reception. I'll promise them that. But I am going to stay the night here, sir. I can tuck in all right on that cot in the corner. They visited mine and the guv'nor's room first, for I went into his on the way to my own and found they had cut open every one of his bags. They had treated my luggage in the same way."

The professor heaved a sigh of relief.

"I shall be glad if you will remain, my boy. You —er —have a way of dealing with these people that is extremely effective."

"I'll give 'em all the lead they want," returned Tinker, with a grin. "And now, sir, you get ready for bed? I am going down to have a few gentle words with the manager, and after that I'll get some things from my own room. I'll leave my pistol with you, and if you hear a sound at either the door or the window, just begin shooting, sir. You will know when I come along, for I shall be whistling."

With that Tinker took his departure.

His interview with the manager could not exactly be described as pleasant, but when he emerged Tinker had a look of deep satisfaction in his eyes, so it was evident that as far as he was concerned he had no kick coming. Then he went to his own room, collected a few things for the night, and went whistling back to the professor.

The latter was already in bed, and as the lad entered he smiled with relief. The big automatic was lying close to his hand, and he handed it back to Tinker.

"No one came, my boy —and, to tell you the truth, I don't know what I should have done if they had, for I have never fired a weapon of any sort in my life."

Tinker smiled, but said nothing. In his mind, however, he was thinking of the professor as a most extraordinary specimen of humanity, for the lad could not conceive of anyone being ignorant of the use of firearms.

He was forgetting that, whereas his own life called for every nerve to be on the alert in case of physical attack, the weapons used by the professor were of a very different sort, and until the occurrence of that strange phenomena at Wadi Abbad nothing but the excitement of some new discovery of the past had ruffled the even tenor of his life.

It was in this state of mind that the lad slipped into his pyjamas and turned out the light. And as he pulled the clothes over him he was thinking inwardly:

"Funniest thing I ever heard! And the old bird is as game as they make 'em. Well, anyway, I'll bet that before we finish this job he knows how to use a gun, or my name is Doughnuts!"

The tall native bowed, and addressed Professor McKenzie in Arabic. "If the effendi is ready, we can leave at once," he announced. "It were better to get away as quickly as possible. There are many reasons." (Chapter 5.)

The Fifth Chapter. Blake in the Background.

AT exactly nine the next morning Professor McKenzie and Tinker were sitting in the glass-enclosed veranda of the hotel. They had finished breakfast half an hour before, and while the professor was smoking a pipe Tinker was on the watch for the man Blake said would appear at nine. Sharp on the hour a "boy" came along to where they were sitting, and behind him strode a tall native, clad in spotless white, and with the eyes and nose of a sheikh rather than of the type of dahabeah captain Tinker had been used to seeing.

Since Tinker's activities of the previous evening, a whisper seemed to have gone round regarding the young Briton, for at breakfast both he and the professor had noticed the cringing manner in which the "boy" had served them; and at every move Tinker made the nearby servants would give a nervous jump as if they expected the young Englishman to pull out his pistol and begin shooting indiscriminately.

The "boy" who was now approaching was no exception. He salaamed most deeply to the professor and Tinker, and then made the announcement that the visitor was asking for Professor McKenzie. He immediately withdrew, and the tall native bowed. He then addressed the professor in Arabic:

"If the effendi is ready we can leave at once," he announced. "The dahabeah is lying close at hand, and everything is on board."

"You are the captain whom I was told would call for us?" asked the professor.

"I am he, effendi. And it were better to get away as quickly as possible. There are many reasons."

The professor turned to Tinker.

"I think it must be he," he said in English. "But I want to make certain."

"This man is all right, sir," he replied. "I'll bet not half a dozen persons besides the guv'nor could have picked such a man. I'm game to trust him to the limit."

And although the tall native gave not the slightest sign that he understood, he knew English as well as his own Arabic, and those words of the young Englishman meant a great deal to him.

"I think so —I think so, my boy," rejoined the professor. Then to the native: "We are all ready, and will go along at once."

34

"It is well, effendi. I have a car waiting, so if you will give instructions about your luggage —"

"I'll do that," said Tinker, springing up. "You go along with the captain, professor."

He hurried away and entered the lounge, where at one side their luggage was waiting —the professor's ordinary bags and the new ones which Tinker had insisted should be delivered to him before eight o'clock that morning. That they had appeared showed the effect of his conversation with the manager the previous evening.

He gave orders for them to be taken out, and, following them, he found the professor and the captain already seated in a large roomy car. There was a second car standing behind the first, into which the luggage was piled, and with a word to the professor Tinker climbed into this. He had no intention of letting the bags out of his sight until they were safely on board the dahabeah.

On reaching the riverside quay where the dahabeah was moored, Tinker soon saw that everything was indeed ready. On the lower deck he could see a number of natives, some of whom he guessed were of the crew, and the others of the labourers Blake had engaged.

He and the professor were conducted to the upper deck, where they found that two large roomy cabins, fitted with electric lights and fans, had been prepared for them. It didn't need more than one swift look round before Tinker knew that the boat Blake had arranged for was certainly no craft belonging to any of the hiring companies or tourist firms. She was far too luxurious in her appointments, and he knew instinctively that she must be the private property of some wealthy Egyptian. How Blake had "wangled" the affair he couldn't guess, but he had seen enough to tell him that the previous week must have been a very busy one for his master.

As he was about to emerge from his cabin an English-speaking native appeared and informed him that he had been assigned to look after him. So Tinker threw him his keys and went out to watch the dahabeah get under way. He was leaning on the rail, looking down at the shrieking mob on the quay, when suddenly his eyes fell on the same red-fezzed native whom he had seen in the lounge at Shepheard's the previous evening just before dinner.

The man was staring at Tinker in the same strange way as before, and although the lad tried his best to return the look with a careless glance, he was again forced to drag his eyes away, for he felt that same strange sensation coming over him. He knew that if he held the other's gaze for even a minute he would be completely hypnotised. And even the first disturbance of his equilibrium was accompanied by an overpowering desire to obey the will behind those eyes.

He stood at the rail, looking everywhere but at the sinister figure. The dahabeah was soon under way, and as she drew clear of the quays she put on more speed. When they had forged ahead it was plain that she had been fitted with superb engines, and that she would be able to make the run in little over half the time employed by other craft.

It was not until they were several hundred yards away that Tinker ventured to gaze back. He saw a figure in the crowd which he opined must be that of the strange native, and as he allowed his gaze to rest on it he knew the other's eyes must be still following him. For even at that distance he felt the stirrings of the same mental disturbance.

Tinker scarcely saw the colourful pageant which they were passing. His thoughts were too deeply absorbed in the strange native who had now disappeared from view.

"He's got some particular interest in our movements," he muttered. "It looks like pretty good betting that he had a hand in the rifling of our luggage last night. Anyway, he wasn't the one I potted. There is a lot about this business that is mighty queer. I'd give something to know just what the guv'nor is up to; but he won't show his hand until he is ready, and my job is to land the professor at Wadi Abbad according to the guv'nor's directions. And if the captain of this dahabeah is as straight as he seems to be I'll guarantee to fulfil my part of the job. But that snaky-eyed bird back there on the quay —I don't like the cut of his jib!

"He knows that we are bound up the river for some spot, and if he is one of the secret society gang who are behind the disappearance of Malone and Rumford, then, if he is out to follow us, he can soon overtake us by train. Well, that's that, and there is nothing else to do for the present. I'll sit tight, keep my eyes open, and my gun handy. That combination ought to keep them from catching me napping."

With that the lad moved along the deck to where the professor was sitting, and, sinking down into a deck chair, he picked up an illustrated English journal.

The dahabeah soon proved her speed. They passed boat after boat on the way up, and a few days later saw them passing Luxor, across from which was the now famous Valley of the Kings, where the late

Lord Carnarvon and Mr. Howard Carter had brought to light the marvellous tomb of Tut-Ankh-Amen.

It was extraordinary to see how little interest Professor McKenzie took in that wonderful discovery. It seemed strange that such a distinguished Egyptologist should have made only one visit to the tomb; but the truth was that every atom of his scientific ego was engrossed in his own work of trying to open up the much older tomb of Menetakhnan, whose wealth he had figured to be far greater than that buried with the Tut-Ankh-Amen of a much later period. For had he not full access to the great gold mines in the south, which for several centuries were lost and then rediscovered by the Queen of Sheba?

They passed Luxor during the early evening, and at dinner the captain entered to inform them that they would reach Wadi Abbad the following afternoon. He added nothing to this brief statement, and the professor and Tinker did not question him.

After dinner they gave orders to have their kit got ready, and Tinker descended to the lower deck to make a final inspection of the working gang. This had been his daily habit on the way up the Nile, and since he spoke Egyptian Arabic fairly fluently, he had little difficulty in making himself understood.

The gang wasn't a bad-looking outfit, and in one of the rare interviews he had had with the captain the latter had told him that each man could be depended on.

It was not until the following afternoon, however, when Wadi Abbad was almost in sight, that the captain came to Tinker's cabin and asked him for an interview. Ever since they had left Cairo the captain had treated Tinker as the senior European of the party; or, rather, the one in charge of all the actual material and personnel, which suited the professor only too well, for it allowed him to spend his entire time poring over his books,

"We shall tie up in about two hours at a small quay close to the spot where the work is to be carried out," announced the captain, when the door was closed. "Those are my instructions from the effendi who engaged me. I have here a letter for you, effendi, which I was ordered to hand to you just before we reached our destination. I shall give it to you now!"

With that the captain thrust a hand inside his white robe and took out an envelope, which he handed to the lad. Tinker saw at the first glance that it was in Blake's handwriting. He tore it open, and scarce noticed that the native had taken his departure. It ran simply:

"This will be handed to you just before you reach Wadi Abbad. The bearer has his instructions. As soon as possible you will get the tents set up and the material ashore. The working gang can remain ashore close to the boat, but it is best that you and the professor should make your quarters on the boat. Things are proceeding fast. I shall be near you all the time, and as soon as it is time to act you will hear from me. Until then, proceed exactly as if you were engaged on the legitimate work of the expedition. It is probable that you will see a certain amount of unusual movement among natives round about Wadi Abbad, for there is a tamasha due soon. I am endeavouring to discover the exact time and place. No more in this —too risky. Explain to the professor. You may trust the captain implicitly. —S. B."

Tinker re-read the letter, then he took out his matchbox and inside a few seconds the paper had been reduced to ashes. He dropped the charred bit on the floor, and rubbed it to dust with his heel; then he went along to see the professor.

They worked their way into the little quay just about two hours later, and although there were no natives to be seen in the immediate vicinity of the spot where the professor and his two companions had previously been at work, Tinker had noted an unusual number during the afternoon. They had been all dressed in feast-day clothes, and apparently bound for a "tamasha " which was about to be held at some spot not far away.

Before dusk a good deal of the material had been landed, and a day tent erected for Tinker and the professor, although they would both sleep on the dahabeah, as Blake had suggested.

With the coming of dusk, Tinker and the professor returned on board and got cleaned up for dinner. It had been decided that from then on they should not "dress," and indeed during the day Tinker had elected to wear khaki shorts. When he was ready, Tinker strolled out on deck and stood by the rail, gazing across to the east where a lovely moon was rising.

As he stood there he was thinking of the distant past when this land that was now desert had been the Queen of the East —when that which was now barren sand had flourished with the rich green of the crops which the people of old had raised, and from which the courts of the Pharaohs drew all their glittering wealth.

It was a long time since Cleopatra; it was a still longer time since Tut-Ankh-Amen had ruled over the land. But it seemed as if the very beginning of time had marked the existence of Menetakhnan, whose tomb, so the professor said, lay in the rough, tumbled heap of rocks —rocks which had lain there how many aeons?

Half dreamily Tinker was listening to the low chatter of the gang of labourers ashore, when suddenly for an instant the great disc of the moon was almost blotted out. As he gazed at it he suddenly became aware that silhouetted against it was the figure of a horseman — animal and burnoused man as still as if carved out of actual stone.

Then Tinker heard a slight sound, and, turning his head, he saw the captain crossing the short gangway to the jetty. He watched him for a few seconds, and saw him pass by the gang of labourers and continue on towards that motionless figure.

For the first time Tinker began to have misgivings.

He was remembering what the professor had said back in Baker Street, how, when he had returned to the camp to try and find some trace of Malone and Rumford, a mysterious horseman had appeared silently and mysteriously, and had made a gesture of anger before disappearing. Could this figure, silhouetted against the moon, be the same?

Then he found that he had lost sight of the captain, but while he was still trying to locate him he saw him suddenly reappear close to the mounted white-clad figure. Tinker narrowed his eyes and watched. He saw the horseman move slightly, and he seemed to bend his head a little. A few moments thus, then suddenly the horse whirled, and the horseman went dashing away into the moon-splashed desert, and the tall figure of the captain could be seen returning to the jetty.

As the native crossed the gang-plank Tinker turned his head a little, but did not speak.

Nor did the captain. He turned and made swiftly for his own quarters, leaving Tinker as mystified as ever. For a moment the lad contemplated going to the captain's quarters and asking him the meaning of the meeting he had just seen. But then he recalled how emphatic Blake had been in both his letters as to the trustworthiness of the man he had selected for the dahabeah, and that made him refrain.

He ate his dinner in silence and then returned to the deck, leaving the professor at work on some notes. As he walked along the captain appeared as if by magic in front of him, and, pausing, said:

"Perhaps the effendi would like to take a stroll on the bank? It is quite safe, and it will be possible to keep everything in sight under the moonlight."

Tinker was about to make some careless form of refusal when, as he gazed shorewards, he thought he saw a mounted figure near the pile of rocks beneath which the tomb was supposed to lay. The moon was then too high to silhouette the mounted man, but Tinker was thinking that it might or might not be the same with whom the captain had talked. In any event, he knew it would be useless to ask the native any questions, so, with a shrug, he said that he might do as the other suggested.

He paced up and down the deck for a few moments, then he came to a decision. He made for his cabin and got his automatic, which he thrust in the side-pocket of his white coat. Then he leisurely made his way on to the jetty and walked past the spot where every man jack of the gang was spread out, fast asleep.

He continued his way in the direction of the great pile of rocks, and as he drew nearer he saw that he had not been mistaken. There was certainly a horseman a little way ahead, and as motionless as the other had been.

Tinker doggedly kept on his way until he was almost up to the mounted man. Still the other didn't move, and out of sheer obstinacy Tinker laid his course so that he might pass close to him. He did so at scarcely two feet distance, and as he was opposite he glanced up into the almost invisible face beneath the burnous.

Then his heart gave a jump, and he stopped in his tracks, for the silent horseman had spoken, and what he said in almost imperceptible tones was:

"Come closer, my lad!"

"Guv'nor!" breathed the lad. The next instant his figure had merged with that of the horse and rider.

As Blake bent downwards Tinker could see that his face was as dark as that of any desert-dweller, and even though he had the voice to assure him that it was indeed Blake, it was even then difficult for him to believe that he was not talking with a real desert Bedouin.

"Listen, my lad. I have already had a talk with the captain. He knows what he has to do. I have been here for some days, and I have discovered many things —the whereabouts of Malone and Rumford for one. I wrote you about a 'tamasha' that was to be held shortly. I have found out only to-day that it is set for to-morrow night, and is being held by an outer circle of the secret Order of Ra.

"Both Malone and Rumford are in their hands, and at the 'tamasha' to-morrow night they will be offered as human sacrifice. Though the men who are giving it are not in the inner circle, some of the higher priests from the inner circle will be present. I do not know the exact spot yet, but hope to find out to-night.

"For the present stand by, but be prepared to hear from me at any time. If we fail to rescue Malone and Rumford to-morrow night all hope of doing so will be gone. These devils haven't had a white sacrifice to offer for years, and on the full of this moon is the annual offering to Menes.

"I am in hiding at an oasis about four miles away, and have been accepted there as a Bedouin, so am all right. But watch out sharp for any message from me. I don't know how it will come, but you will get it before four o'clock to-morrow night. Better turn in and get a good rest. You probably won't get much to-morrow."

"But, guv'nor, can't I do something?" pleaded Tinker.

"Not now. There will be plenty doing to-morrow night. I must leave now, as I have much desert riding and many secret interviews to-night."

Before Tinker had a chance to reply Blake had brought his horse round with a touch at the reins, and the next instant was flying off across the desert, bound on what mission the lad could not guess. He stood until the last faint thud of the hoofs was no longer to be heard, then he returned slowly to the dahabeah and sat down in the shadow to try and figure things out.

"To-morrow night!" he muttered. "All right. The guv'nor says be ready, and I will be! I'd better go along before I turn in, and warn the professor, too,"

Then he sat gazing out across the limitless desert, which could still breed and nourish so much mystery, wondering just what night-riding Blake was doing. But he knew he would have to wait to find that out. So when he had whispered a word in the professor's ear he went into his cabin and got ready for bed.

To-morrow would find him ready.

The whole clamour in the place ceased as the natives saw Menes, the supreme and sacred head of their Order, being bent back slowly in Sexton Blake's relentless grip. (*Chapter 6.*)

A knock on the door of his cabin aroused Tinker early the next morning.

He glanced at his wrist-watch, and saw that it was exactly six o'clock. He called out, and a moment later the door opened to reveal the tall figure of the native captain. He gave a brief salaam, then covered the distance across the cabin in a couple of strides. He took out an envelope which he handed to the lad. Tinker glanced at it, saw that it was addressed to him, and that the writing was Blake's. Then he tore it open and read the contents:

"I have succeeded in discovering what I wanted to know, I am sending this by messenger. I have also written to the captain. Certain reasons make it necessary to drop down-stream during the early morning. The captain will get all the labourers back onboard, and the material. He knows the spot where he is to tie up. Wait for me there. I expect to arrive about nine tonight. —S. B."

Tinker climbed out of his bunk and burned the letter, then, turning to the native, he said:

"You received your letter?"

"Yes, effendi."

"How soon can we get away?"

"In two hours, if the effendi will take charge of the work ashore while I handle things on the boat."

"Good! I'll be out in ten minutes!"

At that the captain withdrew, and, after a quick wash, Tinker climbed into his shorts. He hurried ashore and stirred up the gang, and soon had things on the move. He drank his coffee while he was superintending the work, and it was as nearly two hours as may be when the last line was cleared, and they began to drop down-stream, leaving the spot as barren and deserted as when they reached it the day before.

All the way down Tinker caught occasional glimpses of little groups of natives moving upstream, and he concluded they must form part of the crowd which would attend the "tamasha" that night.

From Blake's letter it seemed that he had succeeded in discovering the spot where the meeting would be held, and as he realised how terribly slim the chances were for rescuing Malone and Rumford his spine went cold. Tinker knew enough of such fanatical gatherings to realise what ghastly tortures would be the portion of the victims before the final sacrifice.

They spent a very quiet day on board the dahabeah. No shore leave was granted to either the crew or the labouring gang. Tinker lounged about his cabin most of the day. As far as he was concerned, he was ready for Blake's arrival, and was impatient for action. Until about four o'clock the day dragged along in deadly fashion. But then Tinker was due to receive one of the biggest surprises of his life.

A few moments after that hour there came a tap on his door, and in response to his voice the door opened to admit the captain of the dahabeah. He closed it carefully after him, then, leaning against it, he drawled in an Oxford accent:

"I fancy I had better disclose my identity now, my lad."

Tinker sat up like a shot and goggled at the tall, dark-skinned man.

"Who —what —" he began.

The other smiled and took a cigarette from under his white jacket.

"So you don't recognise me, even now?" he said. "Well, it speaks a lot for my disguise if it has fooled an expert like you! Don't you know me yet?"

Tinker got up, and, walking across, made a minute examination of the other's features. Then a slow grin spread across his face.

"Is it Mr. Maitland, of the C.I.D.?" he asked hesitatingly.

Maitland, one of the ablest Secret Service men in the East, nodded.

"You've hit it, Tinker! I have been wondering the whole way up if you would spot me."

He sat down and exhaled a heavy cloud of smoke.

"I thought it as well not to disclose my identity until the last moment," he went on.

"I wanted to see what Blake had done before I had a talk with you. But we must have a chat now, in preparation for to-night.

"Listen, my lad. Blake has discovered— or thinks he has discovered —the spot where the big 'tamasha' will be held to-night. For several years now I have been trying to get hold of something definite regarding the secret Order of Ra. I seemed on the point of doing so when the War broke out, and I had no further time to give to it on account of the general unrest in Egypt. But when Blake came to me this time and showed me proof that he was on the track of the outfit, I jumped at the chance to join him.

"Every manjack on board is in the Secret Service —the crew as well as the labourers. And the dahabeah belongs to a wealthy Egyptian, who is loyal to us. Blake has an idea, as I said, where the 'tamasha' will be held, but he will be able to make sure today. At any rate, he will be here by nine, so we shall all be ready.

"We shall not take the crew along with us, but the 'labour gang' will accompany us —fully armed. I don't think it will be necessary to say anything to the professor until just before we start. The old gentleman is greatly exercised over the disappearance of Malone and Rumford, but just now, in the heart of what means life to him, he is absorbed in his calculations. He will come to life to-night all right, when we are ready to start."

Tinker whistled in amazement, and then he grinned. It was a considerable relief to him to know that the famous Maitland was to be of the party, but he was chagrined that he had not spotted him as a European on the way up.

They sat and talked until nearly six, when Maitland took his departure to get his "labour gang" armed and ready for the evening's adventure.

They dined early, and had just gone out on deck when a white-clad figure crossed silently from the bank to the upper deck of the dahabeah. Tinker and Maitland were standing by the rail, and the newcomer came straight towards them. Both knew, of course, that it was probably Blake, and it was. Pausing beside them, he said in a low tone:

"Everything ready?"

Maitland nodded.

"Ready, and waiting for the word," he answered,

"Then we'll get started at once," said Blake. "I have discovered the secret of the meeting."

"Where is it to be held?" asked Tinker and Maitland in one voice.

"I suspected it was to be held somewhere in the neighbourhood of Menetakhnan's tomb, but until this afternoon I didn't know the exact spot. But now I know. Underneath that pile of rocks along the valley exists a secret meeting-place of the Order of Ra. I actually succeeded in gaining an entrance there this afternoon.

"There is no doubt that a very special 'tamasha' is being held to-night, and somewhere down there are Malone and Rumford. Get

Tinker into some sort of native outfit, and then we'll start. I suppose the boat is all ready to make a quick getaway?"

"Steam is up, and we can cast off the moment we are on board."

"Good! I think we had better leave the professor here. In any event, the tomb of Menetakhnan will be a disappointment to him. The secret Order of Ra has had access to, from underneath, for centuries and centuries.

"There is no doubt that it is filled with a vast amount of treasure, and that they have been drawing on it as they needed it. But it is now a case for the Government to seize it, and probably the professor can get himself appointed to take charge of the excavations, which will please him just as well."

"How did the Order get into the tomb?" asked Tinker,

"From their secret chamber underneath. That chamber where the 'tamasha' is being held must have been there when Menetakhnan was buried. But we will talk of that later. Get rigged up, Tinker, and then we shall get along. We have a little time to spare yet, but not much. While you are changing I will have a whisky-and-soda. I am as dry as the desert."

Ten minutes or so later a small group of what appeared to be natives left the dahabeah and crossed to the jetty. From there they took a course up the river in the direction of the barren spot about three-quarters of a mile away where the dahabeah had been tied up the previous day.

In the lead were Blake, Maitland, and Tinker, with the "labour gang" in close formation behind them. They walked at a steady pace until they came near the spot which was their objective.

They saw as they approached that the "tamasha" must indeed be one of a very special nature, for all about the spot were hundreds of natives squatting on the ground, and waiting patiently for a chance to witness as much of the proceedings as possible.

The way which Blake took brought the little party round on the opposite side of the tomb of Menetakhnan, and there the press of the crowd was more dense.

Up to then that side of the great heap of rocks had appeared perfectly blank, but now they could see a shaft of light which seemed to issue from the smooth face of the rock itself. Gently, but always progressing, they worked their way through the crowd until they were only a few feet from the secret entrance, which they could see had been cunningly concealed by a great boulder which looked like any other one of the heaped thousands about them.

The press here was even greater, but Blake and Maitland formed the thin edge of the wedge, with Tinker keeping the gang close up, and in this way their steady pressure gradually cleared a way for them.

They managed at last to reach the threshold, and as they did so they could see that inside it widened out into a sort of vast outer hall.

They pushed through, and found it easier to move once they were within.

Blake turned at once to the left, and they gradually worked their way along towards a wide arch some forty yards away. All heads were turned in this direction, and as they approached closer it was easy enough to guess that the chief ceremony was taking place there.

And as they reached the threshold all three stopped with rage in their hearts at the terrible sight they saw.

THE inner ceremonial room was circular, and about fifty yards in diameter, with a high, vaulted roof.

In the very centre was a pool or bowl some thirty yards in diameter, from which a terrific heat was rising. As the three Europeans craned forward they could see that it was nearly full to the brim with some sort of molten metal, grey in colour, which was bubbling here and there with little sharp pops of exploding steam which sounded evil and sinister in that hole of iniquity.

From the centre rose a stone obelisk on which they could distinguish hieroglyphics; but how far down its base was —how deep the pool —they had no means of knowing. The ten yards space round the place was literally crammed with natives except at two places — one being about half-way round on the right from where the three Europeans stood, and the other about half-way round on the left. In each a square had been railed off for the accommodation of the priests of the Order.

But that was not all that Blake and his two companions saw. It was what had held them petrified as they entered.

In the railed-off square on the left they saw two white men, naked to the waist, and with hands bound behind them. Even at the distance great beads of perspiration could be seen on face and naked torso, and for a moment all three nearly betrayed their true identity by a curse, so enraged were they at the sight of those two lone white men standing on the edge of that terrible pool of boiling metal, and surrounded by a stinking crowd of natives.

Then their eyes turned to the right. In the railed-off square there, which was exactly opposite the other, were gathered half a dozen persons, all clad in rich garments covered with the sacred mystic symbols of the secret Order of Ra. And Sexton Blake knew that the symbols were the same which had been used by the Order at its inception thousands of years before.

Among the group was one tall figure more richly clad than any of the others. In the front of the rich head-dress which he wore were depicted the circle, and the staff and the sacred ibis. At the moment of their entry he had been standing intoning in an expressionless voice some sort of litany of the Order.

Just in front of him stood another priest, and as his eyes fell on him, Tinker gave an audible gasp. He recognised him as the same man he had seen twice in Cairo, and who had gazed at him in such sinister fashion.

The creature's eyes were fixed on the two white men across from him.

Rumford was undoubtedly in a state of hypnotic quiescence, for he was standing a couple of feet back from the edge of the pool. But Lawrence Malone was already moving along at the hypnotic command of the evil thing in human form, and inch by inch he was approaching the edge of the pool.

Tinker was horrified at the horrible sight. A few more shuffling steps, and nothing could save Lawrence Malone from stepping off into the terrible bubbling mass of boiling metal.

He had given only a cursory glance at the tall priest who was speaking, but Sexton Blake had recognised him at once as Prince Menes, the head of the Order. As he glimpsed what was afoot he knew that they must act at once if they were to save Malone and Rumford.

He turned to Maitland, and said swiftly:

"Take your men and get through to Malone and Rumford. Tinker and I will make for the gang of priests. Our only hope is to break that spell before Malone goes over."

Then, touching Tinker's arm, he started round the right-hand side of the place, pushing his way through without a word, kicking a native out of his way here, and hurling one aside there. So intent were the priests on their work, and so engrossed the mob of natives, that for some little time their passage was scarcely noticed. But when Blake and Tinker were within half a dozen feet of the enclosed space where Menes stood, the latter turned his head, and his eyes met Blake's full.

Despite the disguise that Blake had assumed, he knew that Menes had pierced it. He turned his head and gave a quick look across the pool, and saw that Maitland and his men were close to the spot where Malone and Rumford stood.

Then, with a sharp word to Tinker, Blake rushed ahead.

He covered the railing in a leap, and landed close behind the evil creature who was dragging Malone inch by inch to a terrible death. At the same moment Menes gave a shout, and, turning, rushed at Blake, with the other priests closing in after him.

Blake was not loath to come to grips, but he knew that first he must, at any cost, make the key move that would stop Malone.

He dodged the first rush, therefore, leapt to one side, and kicked out with all his strength.

He caught the man who had hypnotised Malone full in the back, and there arose a terrible scream as the creature plunged into the pool of boiling metal. That had been the only hope, and even as he came to grips with Menes, Blake was able to see Maitland and his men dragging Malone and Rumford back from the edge of that hell.

For with the perishing of the hypnotist the spell had been broken. Though dazed and bewildered to find themselves in such a place, both the explorer and the financier were soon in the normal possession of their senses, although Blake was far too busy to notice that.

At the first impact Blake had driven in a terrific body blow that had caught Menes full over the heart. The Egyptian had stopped as if a ram had hit him, but only for a moment and in the next few minutes Blake discovered that part of the extraordinary life's training given to Menes had included a very comprehensive, training in the fighting methods of the weak.

The bevy of priests behind him, while knowing nothing of this manner of fighting, were not at a loss.

From beneath their gorgeous robes one and all drew long knives, and while some made for Tinker the rest rushed to the assistance of Menes.

Standing back, Tinker coolly took a couple of pot-shots. One brought down the nearest priest to himself, and the second caught one who was rushing towards Menes just as he was passing the edge of the pool. There was a great cry as he threw up his arms and flung the knife high. The next instant he toppled over and had disappeared beneath the seething grey molten metal.

Then Tinker changed his position a little, and shouted in Arabic:

"One step, and the rest of you get the same!"

They halted and drew back, while Blake and Menes had most of the space to themselves.

By some sort of chance each had abandoned their first method of fighting, and were now interlocked in a terrific wrestling hold.

Out of the corners of his eyes Tinker could see that a battle royal was going on across the pool, but he dared not look directly, for he knew the second he relaxed his vigilance the priests would rush him.

He was leaving Blake to himself, for he had no fear as to the final outcome. But it came sooner than even he expected.

Suddenly the whole clamour in the place ceased on a high-pitched wail that was cut off sharply as the crowd of natives saw Menes, the sacred and supreme head of their Order, being bent back slowly, inch by inch, as Sexton Blake forced him down and down and down towards the sheer edge of the pit.

From where he stood, Tinker could see that the prince's face had turned to grey, and the sweat was standing out in great beads on his forehead as that remorseless grip which Blake had secured left him helpless to do aught but brace himself as much as the agony would let him.

He knew it was hopeless, and Blake knew he had his man where he wanted him. But the onlookers knew nothing of that until, with a shrill scream, Menes' resistance broke and he crashed to the stone kerbing, his face hanging out over the bubbling metal beneath. No one knew better than he what awaited the human being who plunged into that cauldron.

Holding him thus, Blake bent down, and rasped:

"You've got one chance, Menes —and only one! Raise your voice and order this gang out of the place. But before you give the order charge them that my companions and myself are not to be molested. You dirty hound, if anything had happened to Malone or Rumford I'd have sent you into that pool as I sent the other one.

"Maitland of the police is across there with twenty of his men, and you know what it means if you refuse! Now, give the word! If you don't hasten, over you go!"

And Blake accompanied the threat by a stiffening of his hold and a slight pushing of Menes nearer the edge.

But Menes had had enough.

Slowly and in a muffled voice he gave instructions to the crowd of natives, word for word as Blake dictated, and, as if by magic, they began to make for the entrance-way. In fact, so eager were they —so in fear of the strange proceedings of that night —that they jostled in a state of panic, and there came scream after scream as one after another was pushed into the terrible pool which greedily took them into its maw.

For ten minutes the place was a bedlam of terror. Then, as the last group fought its way frantically through to freedom, Blake released his hold of Menes and rose.

"Thanks, my lad!" he said, drawing his own automatic. "That was exactly what I wanted you to do."

Then he gazed across the pool where he could see Maitland, Rumford, and Malone coming round the kerbing, followed by Maitland's men.

"Wait at the exit, Maitland!" he called, and once more turned to Menes.

"I don't know yet what I am going to do about this devil's business you were up to to-night," he said slowly, "I have been wondering what you were up to during the last four or five years. What is done rests with the police, and that is Maitland's end of it. But one thing I will tell you —every shred of devil's fixings down here is going to be cleaned out. And until it is the whole bunch of you are coming as our prisoners. Now give the word to your crew, then march towards the exit."

Menes hesitated for an instant; then, with a half-smile on his lips, he muttered a command to the other priests and obeyed.

As they reached the exit both Blake and Tinker were overwhelmed by Malone and Rumford, for Maitland had already told them to whom they owed their delivery.

Then, with Menes and his companions marshalled before them, they passed through the big outer chamber and through the narrow slit in the rock to the outer air.

On emerging they looked round for the natives who had been there such a short time before. But not a single one was to be seen. They had vanished as if by magic. Had they not actually already seen them it would have been difficult to believe that the whole thing was not some fantastic dream.

●　　　●　　　●　　　●　　　●

There is little more to tell of that meeting of Blake's with Prince Menes after those years during which he had lost track of the Egyptian.

Neither Malone nor Rumford could give a coherent explanation as to what had happened when the violet dome of light had exploded over them. It must have hurled them down unconscious, for the next they remembered was coming to their senses in a small rough stone cell, which they guessed was underground. But until that night they did not know that it was beneath and close to the tomb of Menetakhnan, which they had sought to discover.

Maitland took charge of the prisoners, and on his arrival in Cairo handed them over to the Egyptian police. And a month or so later Sexton Blake knew why Menes had given a half-smile when he had obeyed that order at the edge of the pool of boiling metal.

It was when he and Tinker were back in London that they had a letter from Maitland telling them that Menes had escaped, and adding that it was no more than he had expected, for no man can comprehend the workings of the wheels within wheels in the East.

Nor was Blake surprised, for he knew how little chance there had been to get a conviction against the prince, for there would be many who would be among his followers (secretly), and who looked upon him as sacred.

As for Professor McKenzie, he was greatly disturbed to find that such events had been taking place while he had remained on board the dahabeah in ignorance; but he was somewhat mollified when, through Maitland's influence, he was promised that when the Government should decide to begin excavations at Wadi Abbad on its own behalf he should be placed in charge of the work.

But Sexton Blake knew how little prospect there was of that promise being fulfilled, and when he heard it Tinker simply grinned; then his face grew serious, for he was remembering that terrible night on the edge of the pool of boiling metal, above which lay Menetakhnan, twin-brother of the first Prince Menes.

THE END.
[21500 WORDS]

A Story of the Years to Come— And of the Power of the Atom.

TO REMIND YOU—
The Atom Smashers
By L. H. Robbins

A Story of the Years to Come— And of the Power of the Atom.

(It is notable that the author of this serial has only one reference in the encyclopedic 'philsp' website and no mention in the WorldCat.Org catalogue. /drf)

AMERICA, in the year 1940, is in the grip of two gigantic forces. One is a vast revolutionary organisation of militant industrial terrorists, calling themselves the "Red Eyes," or "Irresistibles," and the other is the newly-discovered power of the Atom —the result of years of research, in which the scientists of our own day are even now engaged.

A man thought to be Colonel Allen Derwin is killed in an explosion attributed to the "Red Eyes." Paul Mercer, a young newspaper-man, discovers that the dead man is not Derwin, but an imposter killed in mistake.

The colonel, the "big" man in American finance, desires to keep his continued existence a secret. His object is to defeat the Red Eyes. Paul helps him in this by taking Derwin's wife and daughter to the safety or their country home. Paul returns to the city, where Derwin is conferring with other financiers about fighting the new menace.

Jules Manton, another magnate, is present, and confesses to having had an interview with the man who made the attempt on Derwin's life. He carried a blue leather box, chained to his wrist, and threatened that if he was attacked he would destroy the building.

(Now read on.)

The Council of War.

"HIS talk was so wild that when he asked me if I didn't think him a lunatic," I answered, 'Yes.' The man was certainly on the ragged edge of insanity, yet there was something in his manner —decision or self-confidence or just pure devilry —that made me listen to him.

"He started to tell me the stuff in the letters that you, colonel, have been getting. I told him I knew it all and was willing to concede his claims.

"To quiet him and get the upper hand of him in the rapid-fire conversation that he was pulling, I told him that I knew a dozen cranks who were working on his subject, I let him know that I was up on the theory of atomic activity, and that I was ready to risk a little money either in buying his invention outright or in backing him in further experiments.

"He was pleased as a child. All his type are, easily flattered, as you know.

"And he showed me the thing. I have seen it, gentlemen. I have looked at the infernal machine that has the drop on the world to-day. For that is precisely the situation. I am convinced that nothing on earth can stand up in front of that machine.

"He laid the blue leather case on the table, unfastened the straps, and took out the invention. The chain came out with it, so it was the gun, not the case, that was linked to his arm.

"You may call it a gun if you like, but it looked to me, as nearly as I can describe it, like a brass camera, with a brass nozzle at the front end of it and a glass lens in the mouth.

"The way he fondled it, you'd have thought it was a prize kitten, and he called it 'Little Brazenose.' I can't tell you much about it in detail, except that there was a black rubber handle at the back, and the body was yellow brass, with two or three small, round glass buttons projecting from the sides; and there were wires —insulated wires. I remember these features distinctly.

"And the brass parts had evidently been made by hand by a skilled workman; in fact, there was nothing amateurish about it. The thing made me think, as I say, of a camera —a finely constructed and high-priced machine for taking snapshots. An assassin using it in a crowded street would scarcely be noticed."

Manton paused to mop the sweat from his brow. The attitude of the other men in the room, Mercer noticed, had softened towards him. The stout Campbell Duguid no longer glared accusingly but bent forward upon the table edge, listening eagerly.

"Don't take it so hard, Manton," spoke Allan Derwin. "You did what the rest of us should have done, as I now see. You've seen him and seen his invention —"

"And I've seen him work it!" cried Manton.

The Gun.

"I'VE seen him work it. For after I had looked at it and admired it, stringing the idiot along, you know, I played the idiot myself by telling him he would have to give me a demonstration. 'You promised to demonstrate your instrument to Colonel Allan Derwin yesterday,' I told him. 'Evidently Derwin wasn't impressed.'

"At that my man went to raging and cursing. He said you had played fast and loose with him, sir; you had disappointed him in failing to meet him at Grand Central.

"And then he made the astounding statement which I ask you all to take into account when you judge my conduct since yesterday morning.

"He said that all men who saw the gun work were thereafter his deadly enemies, except upon one condition; and that condition was abject subservience to his will. The man's plumb crazy, you see."

Spoke Campbell Duguid:

"I'm not so sure he is as daft as you think. The nature of his invention makes him an outlaw, an enemy of all mankind. The law of self-preservation dictates that his ethics must be those of the rattlesnake. He has enough sense to know it."

"Right," said Lambeth Dunn. "He can't peddle his machine around until he finds a buyer, for the customer who won't buy it is bound to be a betrayer and a prosecutor. I begin to see why he tried to kill the colonel. If he didn't exterminate our friend here, our friend would exterminate him."

"That's the way he put it up to me, as I sat helpless in front of him, with the brass nose of the thing pointing at me," said Manton, shivering. "He had been standing near a window. He turned suddenly to face it, and he said: 'Look here, if you want a demonstration.'

"And, gentlemen, before I could fall upon him, he had aimed the camera thing out the window and down across Broadway at the Metals Building; and swift as a cat he touched one of the glass buttons —and the whole town rocked with the explosion that instantly followed."

Boiling with wrath, Jules Manton rose and began to pace the floor before his audience, continuing on his feet to the conclusion of his tale.

"I laid him out flat, of course," said he. "I smashed him in a heap in the corner. But while I grabbed for a paperweight to brain him with, he came right-side up and sat there aiming the brass box at me and grinning like —like nothing but the devil.

"'Before you make another move,' said he, in the squeaky voice that he has, 'take time to think whether you want a dose of what I have just now given your great and good friend Allan Derwin. For I have killed Derwin,' he said. 'Something else seems to have happened, also. What it was I don't know. I guess I shot a steam boiler somewhere.'

"Well, I cursed him with every foul word I could lay my tongue to, but he just sat there on the floor, aiming the grinning; and, gentlemen, for once in my life I was a coward. He had me. And still I didn't believe what he said about Derwin.

"Your invitation to call here this morning has served me a double purpose,' he said. 'I have interested you in my little invention, and I have also put out of the way a man who refused to be interested in it.' 'You've killed Allan Derwin?' I cried. 'Look across the way,' he answered. 'You know his office. Look and see. I have killed him as I will kill you unless you decide to back me with your money and your protection. If you decline, I shall have to put you aside and hunt another market.'

"Well, I couldn't believe. There had been no flash, no sound from the brass box; and yet I knew from the roar of the explosion and the racket of the fire-engines in the street, that he had done some frightful damage. And while I stood murdering him in my mind, he got up, dusted his clothes, and said to me:

"I suppose I ought to kill you now. But it wouldn't be good business. It might be killing an easy customer. I'd like nothing better than to turn Little Brazenose loose on you to play you back for the smash you handed me. And do you know,' here he grinned harder than ever —'do you know what you'd die of if I did?

"'You'd die of cancer —instantaneous and all-consuming cancer. That's what Little Brazenose does to people he don't like. He devours 'em alive. And they think they're burned. Oh, I know! We've had some accidents in our laboratory.

"But, I don't blame you a lot for smashing me,' he went on 'after what I did to your friend across the way. Any man would have lost his head under the circumstances. So I'll let bygones be bygones, Mr. Manton; and I hope when I see you again you'll be in a more amiable frame of mind.'

"With that he walked to the door, picking up the blue leather case on the way. I hoped he would put the gun inside it, in which case I meant to smear him before he reached the elevator. But he didn't. He tucked the brass thing under his arm and swung the case over his shoulder by a strap, and he said:

"I let you live because you are the sort of man I've been looking for. You're not one of these new-fangled, Golden Rule magnates like Derwin.

"You're a roughneck, though you wear fine clothes. You'd like to own this pretty machine of mine to use against the anarchists. You see its merits, where our humane friend across the street was grieved and shocked. Oh, I know, you Manton! And you'll come to me, I think.'

"He had his hand on the doorknob and still he stayed. 'My price is not high,' he said. 'I want a million dollars in United States gold — not much— just enough to support me in my old age, which is almost here, and to take care of anybody who may be dependent upon me.

"There are certain details —for example, I shall have to be well out of the country with my gold in my baggage before you will come into possession of Little Brazenose. But we can discuss those matters later. The immediate thing is this.'

"And, gentlemen, I'll say that he quit talking like a wild man and became thoroughly businesslike.

"He said: 'I will give you a week to make up your mind. In the course of the week, watch the papers. You will read of certain doings which you will recognise as being demonstrations intended for you. I hope they will influence you to decide right.

(Another instalment next week! Doesn't this yarn seem to be the real serial stuff?)

www.ingramcontent.com/pod-product-compliance
Lightning Source LLC
Chambersburg PA
CBHW020339130626
46549CB00003B/1218